OTHER BOOKS BY ANNA JONES:

Haven

A WORLD AWAY

A Novel

ANNA JONES

Covenant Communications, Inc.

Covenant

Cover painting *The Gadfield Elm Chapel* © Al Rounds.
For information on prints by Al Rounds, call Al Rounds Studio at (801) 261-4518.

Cover design © 2001 Covenant Communications, Inc.
Published by Covenant Communications, Inc.
American Fork, Utah

Printed in the United States of America
First Printing: April 2001

07 06 05 04 03 02 01 00   10 9 8 7 6 5 4 3 2 1

ISBN 1-57734-817-6

To my friends

$\mathcal{G}$LOSSARY AND
PRONUNCIATION GUIDE

ar werth *(are weorth; "th" is pronounced as in "thank")* for sale

bara brith *(barra breeth)* literally "spotted bread"; a traditional fruit loaf

croeso *(croy-soh)* welcome to haven

cwn bach ar werth *(koon bäch are weorth; the "ch" is aspirated as in German)* puppies for sale

hafan *(hav-ann)* haven; a place of peace, safety, and tranquility

iechyd da *(yě ch d ĭdah; the "ch" is aspirated as in German)* good health or cheers

nain *(nine)* grandmother

os gwelwch chi'n dda *(ŏs gooě looch chěn thah; "th" is pronounced as in "the")* please

pob bendith *(pawb bendeth; "th" is pronounced as in "thank")* every blessing (to you)

samphire *(sam fir)* edible seaweed/herb which grows on rocks in certain areas along the British coastline

NOTE

In the Welsh language words may change their first letter when they follow certain other words (which makes it an extremely difficult language to learn—or to look up in a dictionary!). For example, the Welsh say **Croeso** (welcome) and **Cymru** (Wales) *but* **Croeso i Gymru** (welcome to Wales). The emphasis in a word always falls on the penultimate syllable (i.e., the first syllable in a two-syllable word), which also makes it a very rhythmic and poetic language.

$\mathcal{P}$ROLOGUE

The mountains stretched ahead across the horizon, tall and sharp. They seemed impassable, but for the narrow gray road that slipped cautiously between them, twisting through rocky outcrops on its way further and deeper into the range.

It was like a fortress, she thought, and her fearful heart was inspired by the sudden notion that these inhospitable peaks were a barrier between her and the agony she'd left behind. It was cold and wild up here, but warm in the car; the music from the radio was light and comforting.

Belinda looked around quickly to check once again on her dear boy, asleep in the backseat, his long, delicate eyelashes brushing his porcelain cheeks. Just for a moment she felt as if she could stop the car and climb into the backseat beside him, then pull her knees into her chest and feel the old security she had enjoyed as a child hiding under warm heavy blankets. They were almost safe. They would be far away soon.

She had driven through the night without stopping. Just as they crossed the border, an early dawn had broken, giving her enough light to appreciate their beautiful surroundings and to read the smaller, unlit signs at the side of the road. That gave her yet more comfort, seeing how different the majestic and mountainous scenery was here from the flat industrial land which she had fled. The major road signs displayed two languages, but the smaller signs here bore only one: Welsh. She guessed, from the Estate Agency boards outside several houses, that *Ar Werth* meant for sale; but the sight of a hand-painted stake outside one home offering *Cwn Bach Ar Werth* gave no indication whether it referred to home-grown vegetables or puppies.

While growing up in the south of England, Belinda had always wanted to visit Wales, although she could not pinpoint exactly when or why this desire had begun. Family holidays during her childhood had inevitably been to Norfolk or Southport, where her family had relatives who could put them up cheaply, and she had often yearned to visit this land of ancient castles, bracing beaches, and proud traditions. Leaving the confines of her family to marry the enigmatic and charming Marty Hunt, she had hoped for so much. She thought she might at last see the realization of her dreams, which had often been scorned by her unambitious and disinterested parents.

A year into their marriage, Belinda had asked him whether they might take a short break together in the Brecon Beacons in the south of Wales, and his refusal had been the first of the many disappointments which had come to characterize their relationship. Hunched over the wheel of the car, she caught her breath as she remembered having once told him of her wish to go to Wales. Would he remember? She could not afford to leave him any clues as to where she might go.

This was probably far enough, she decided eventually, comforted to know that her long journey was almost at an end. Welcome though the thought was, however, it brought with it only more unknowns. Where would she and her son sleep tonight? How long before they were forced to move on again? Would the money last until she could find a job, somewhere to settle? She had become used to living with fear, but this was a fear she had never faced before—fear of what was ahead, of the future. A few moments of pain and humiliation were somehow more bearable than the prospect of poverty, shame, and ultimate failure.

In the back seat Jake still lay sleeping, his face peaceful, revealing a perfect childish certainty that his mother knew what she was doing and would keep him safe. She had to be strong for her son. She looked to the mountains again and imagined them a great fortress, a natural barrier between her and all she had left behind. Here in the wild isolation of Wales, far from everything she had known, she could draw breath, get ready to start again, be safe.

As if on cue, a sign caught her attention, and she gazed at it with desperate relief, suddenly aware of how emotionally and physically exhausted she was, and just how badly she needed the rest and safety the sign represented. She pressed a heavy foot onto the brake and wrenched the steering wheel round, shifted into second gear, and began to climb the steep, graveled driveway alongside the slate sign that read, "Haven—Bed and Breakfast."

CHAPTER 1

Gwen Anderton imagined, as she watched the valley arrayed beneath her windows, that she could see the gradual movement of the shadows as they drew back from the lifting sun now reflected in the lake. She watched the newly shorn sheep, munching industriously yet contentedly, their bare skin warmed by the early morning rays. There was little she loved more than to spend a peaceful moment dwelling on the wonder and beauty of the world that surrounded the stone farmhouse. Each morning might be fresh and new to her as though she had never seen it before, as she looked out across the valley and pondered on the meaning of eternity and her wonderful blessings.

Her reverie was disturbed by the sight of a red van creeping noisily up the graveled path, and she smiled warmly, raising a hand in silent greeting in case the postman had observed her presence. She was a little embarrassed that he might have noticed her, thinking she was awaiting an important letter. Admittedly she was, but the postman could not know that it had become her practice to spend a little time each day meditating on the beauty of the scenery that surrounded Haven while her new husband took care of some of the work that had once been hers alone. It was by chance today that those precious minutes had coincided with the postman's arrival.

The letters dropped onto the mat with a satisfying thud, and she picked them up tentatively. The envelope she had expected was there.

She was happy to note a second letter as well, this one in an airmail envelope postmarked "Salt Lake City" and bearing a return address that thrilled and delighted her. It was possible, thought Gwen, that the pleasure of making the final plans for her visit to the United States to be sealed in the temple might alleviate some of the bitterness that the other letter would almost certainly bring.

"Was that the post?"

She had not heard Edward enter, but her heart leapt in gladness at seeing him, as it always did. He took the first letter from her willing hands and put a comforting arm around her shoulder as he read it. It was from Edward's daughter, Angela. Hurriedly written, which they might have expected and would certainly overlook, it was also curt and brusque in tone, which Edward could not forgive. Angela and her family would indeed be visiting them, she confirmed, though it was clear from her choice of words that it was only at his insistence that she and her family were coming to Haven and they did not expect to enjoy their visit. Not only was the letter rude, Edward noted, it was also late. Angela, her husband, and their three children planned to arrive that very evening. It was fortunate that Gwen had deliberately kept the family bedroom available for the last few weeks, even though she had lost a considerable amount of income by doing so.

For a moment Edward felt an uncharacteristic anger at his daughter's attitude. He had excused her often enough both to Gwen and to himself. Their marriage had been rather sudden, Angela didn't really know Gwen yet, she was only being loyal to her mother's memory, she was tired because of the baby . . . but for all Edward's reasoning the fact remained that Angela hated Gwen. He had tried to protect his new wife from that truth, but she was an intelligent woman. She could not help but realize that her stepdaughter disliked her.

"Well," Gwen sighed, "I'd better go and get their room ready then. Have you finished the invoices?"

He blushed as he admitted that he had not, and she smiled, knowing that he, too, had been nervous, waiting for Angela's letter. He had duties, he reminded himself. The bills had to be prepared. Gwen had always hated to ask her guests for money, she had told him. Over the days that her guests stayed in her home, she often came to know them very well. In fact, the time they spent was so personal, that she felt it was almost impolite and inappropriate to ask them for money just as they were saying good-bye. But Edward had willingly taken that responsibility from her, and many more, and in doing so had found his place at Haven. Now, only weeks into their marriage, it was as though he had always belonged here, at her side.

In some respects, he thought to himself, he *had* always belonged here. Now that he was here, his entire body exulted with the contentment of certainty that this was the path intended for him. His former life, a hundred miles away in Birmingham, might have been a hundred years ago. He had left his suburban bungalow full of memories of his late wife, Edith, to take his rightful place at Gwen's side. He was happier here than he had ever imagined possible.

But his new life was not entirely without its difficulties. It was because he had been married before that he knew how difficult the earliest months could be as two people struggled to adjust to sharing every part of their lives and compromising their independence. His dear Gwen had been surprised to discover just how much awkwardness there could be between them as they expressed differing opinions on which brand name they preferred, or how late either might wish to read in bed, or which radio station they would listen to. She had been distressed in the first month of their marriage when he asked why she had changed the telephone company without talking to him about it. He recognized how difficult it must be for her to remember to include him in everything, when she had lived alone for so long. In turn, Gwen had been upset at the realization that their marriage would not always be perfect and that it was actually more difficult than she had imagined. But together they were learning, and with time it would grow easier.

There were changes for him too, not just the little sacrifices that were inherent in a new marriage, but the gradual shift in perspective and understanding brought about by the close intertwining of their recent union and his only slightly less recent conversion to the LDS faith. He had always known that Gwen's beliefs were the basis of her life and that they shaped her personality and actions. But now, as he adjusted to a new routine of daily study and prayer together, frequent church meetings and weekly family home evenings, he began to feel as an exchange student might, thrust headfirst into a strange culture that he had up until this point known only from books.

During the weeks he had studied the gospel with missionaries, first here at Haven and then at home in Birmingham, he had tried to separate his feelings for Gwen from his feelings about the gospel. He had known from the very beginning that if he were to reject what he was being taught, their relationship would have to end since Gwen had vowed in her youth only to marry a man who shared her beliefs. Their tentative romance was acceptable to her only because he was learning about the gospel. But he had also known that it would be deeply hypocritical and unfair to both of them if he were to accept baptism just so that he could marry the woman he had loved for five years, ever since her sympathy and compassionate understanding at his wife's premature death had warmed his heart.

During the two lessons he had had with Elder Nelson and Elder Mullins at Haven, he had found it nearly impossible to dissociate Gwen and her faith in his mind. She had beamed radiantly at him as the plan of salvation was outlined, and their newly declared affection for one another was uppermost in his mind as he returned her smile.

When he returned to Birmingham, two more missionaries had come, and this time he had tried to concentrate entirely on what they told him and forget that Gwen formed part of the equation at all. He had even tried to make himself question what he heard, buying anti-Mormon pamphlets from a local Christian bookshop, although he found that most of the arguments presented in them seemed spurious at best and often ridiculous, even to his untrained mind.

A loving telephone call from Gwen one evening, two weeks after he had returned from Haven, had brought the memory of her goodness and bright spirit rushing back to his mind. Later, in his bedroom he had picked up his Book of Mormon, which he was already partway through reading, and reminded himself with all the strength he could muster not to give in because of Gwen but to hold on to his doubts. The answer came from his own mind in an immediate reply: "What doubts?"

From that moment he began to realize that he really did understand and believe to his core all that he was learning about the restored gospel. His baptism had taken place only days later, and Gwen had attended. He had embraced her afterwards with a new joy and a sure knowledge that he would have taken this life-changing step even without her influence.

It was so different, however, learning a new faith at his own pace as a widower in his own home, to practicing it fully as a new couple. It was so much easier being a new convert in a large ward, which had nurtured him and answered questions before they were asked. Now, in the Nefyn Branch, he was one of only five local priesthood holders, all deeply respected and frequently consulted by the members of the tiny branch. It wasn't until after his marriage that he had suddenly realized how little he knew of the philosophy he had adopted. On their wedding day Gwen had tenderly whispered to him, "I know you have always been dear to me, even before this life," and he had puzzled for a few moments until he remembered that the premortal existence was part of his new belief system.

He picked up the pile of invoices he'd left on the table, and saw that he had written nothing on them, so lost was he in his thoughts. He was startled when Gwen's gentle teasing voice sighed, "I wish we didn't have to charge them anything, too, my darling, but we must make a living."

He turned his head to her and kissed her cheek warmly. "I was just thinking how much my life has changed in the last few months." Seeing the questioning look, he added with a smile, "For the better."

"I just hope Angela will realize that," Gwen said, the spiteful letter still weighing heavily on her mind. Edward saw thick tears form in her eyes and grasped her hand. He held it until she raised her eyes to his, and with that motion a tear was dislodged and began its path down her pale cheek.

He tried to speak reassuringly. "It's going to be a difficult week for us, my love. But we'll get through it. It'll be fine. You'll see."

Gwen pressed her eyes closed for a moment, and when they opened, they were a little clearer, more hopeful. She had been praying, he knew. She often did that, as though it were second nature to offer a quick silent prayer about anything, whether it troubled or delighted her. "Of course we will," she said, and meant it. Still seeing some doubt in the furrows in his brow, she kissed him reassuringly.

CHAPTER 2

Bright red neon letters burned into Marty Hunt's still-hazy mind with an insistence that was somehow strange. It seemed more forceful than usual, despite the fact that it had long been his habit to awaken with the square red numbers of the radio alarm inches from his similarly tinted eyes. They read "8:30." Nothing unusual there. He had not yet raised his head from the pillow, but on the periphery of his vision all was not as it should have been.

No headache, he noted with satisfaction. It had been a good night, what he remembered of it. He was a strong man who could take his drink and never suffer any after effects. His mind still had some difficulty concentrating, but the cloudiness would pass, he knew from experience. Another drink often helped clear things up again. Still, there was something wrong . . .

He sat up slowly, carefully, and in doing so caught sight of his reflection in the dressing-table mirror opposite. A two-day growth of stubble—women liked that rough and ready look, he knew. Although his hair was tousled and his face slightly puffy with sleep, he was a fine, good-looking man, he told himself. It had been a good night last night. Paul had been in great form, putting some chap to rights about . . . something to do with politics, he couldn't quite remember what. His brother, Paul, always managed to have the right answer and to say it very loud, and that always won any altercation.

Still something wrong, though. Marty debated getting up, then fell back down and rolled over to the other side of the bed, the sweet-smelling side where the pillows were always plumped up. A detective novel and glass of cold water always stood neatly on the bedside table. In the drawer he knew he would always find a pocket-sized packet of tissues, some pills, hand cream, nail clippers, and a little diary and pen. His wife was so organized, everything just so, which was as it should be with women, so he supposed he couldn't complain.

He dozed for half an hour, knowing there was no point in getting up just yet. He could manage without a cigarette for a while longer. But even his light dreams were troubled by that nagging feeling that all was not well, and at last he sat up and looked around in confusion, wondering what his subconscious had noticed that the rest of him had not.

It seemed all right. He had half expected to find himself on Paul's sofa again, but no, he was in his own bedroom, decorated in the horrible floral stuff that Lindy had chosen years ago. And there was his wallet, safe where he had put it, money and betting slips intact and untouched. Despite the gloom, he could just make out the gold watch Paul had given him on the floor by his clothes. It settled his mind to see everything all right there at least.

It was the fact that he could barely see his watch that finally made him realize what was wrong. The curtains were still closed. Some light was finding its way into the room but not enough to help him wake up fully. What was Lindy thinking of? She always threw the curtains open at eight o'clock, as he had told her to, and she always brought him a cup of coffee and tried to wake him and persuade him to get up for work. Where was his coffee? Late again.

He got out of the bed and cast his eyes around for the rest of his clothes. As he thumped the light switch, the sudden bright light made him blink and wakened him further, so that he finally started to notice what else was wrong. Never mind the curtains and his "cuppa"—what had Lindy done with everything? Her makeup case was gone from the dressing table; the novel he was so used to seeing was gone from her bedside. When he opened the wardrobe door to look for his clean jeans, he saw that her clothes were gone, all of them, every last item.

Beginning to feel angry and outraged, he nearly ran to the top of the staircase to bellow out her name. There came no timid reply, no light feet rushing on the stairs, just the echo of his own voice and then the strange displaced sound of a bell ringing. It startled him for a moment before his otherwise occupied brain placed it as the telephone and sent him to answer it.

"Marty. Paul." The two brothers always greeted one another in this fashion.

"Paul, hi. Lindy's gone. She's left me."

There was stunned silence for a few seconds as his brother took in this news.

"When?"

"Don't know. I just woke up and she's gone. Looks like she's taken my boy with her, too." His mind was still woolly from a night's drinking, which had ended only a few hours ago, but it was just dawning on him that he hadn't heard anything of little Jake's usual morning cacophony.

"So you don't know where she'll have gone, then?" Paul asked.

"I'll try ringing her mother's. Don't suppose she's there, though." Now that the truth had filtered through the haze that surrounded his mind, he was angry at the presumption of his quiet little wife. Imagine her thinking she could just leave like this, abandon him, and steal the son he was working so hard to mold in his own image. "She's no right to go!" he spat angrily. "She belongs here!"

Paul was still stunned, but quickly becoming as angry as his brother. "She can't do this to you. She just can't! We'll get her, mate. We'll get her back, and your little lad, too." There was venom in his voice, the sort which Marty knew terrified Lindy, but which he admired so much because it meant that Paul would follow through, would win, would get his way. Nothing stopped Paul when he was angry.

Marty himself was calmer in his fury. He could have torn his wife apart at that moment, but he would never show it. He was a cool customer, all right. Looking at himself in the mirror, he cocked his head to one side and narrowed his eyes. Yes, a cool customer.

"Thanks Paul. You're a good man to have for a brother. We'll get them back, both of us somehow, one way or the other, we'll get them. She can't do this to me. We'll bring her in, dead or alive."

The bed and breakfast looked to be an old stone farmhouse, and it was actually quite plain, an indication, she hoped, that the rates would be reasonable. She had to make her money last until she found work.

She turned off the engine and sat a moment, gathering strength. Jake was still asleep and she would need to wake him up and unload the car. Studying the bed and breakfast, she saw that it was built of the same gray stone and slate as the earlier homes she had passed, but its defensive position on the mountainside and its great age endowed it with an air of eternity and of refuge. The colorful and neatly tended gardens surrounding it helped create a warmth and homeliness that lifted her spirits.

She supposed Marty must have realized by now that she was gone, not that he had paid her much attention when she had been there. He barely noticed her in the morning, wanting only his coffee, and since he was invariably late for work, he was always late coming home. On Friday evenings he tended not to come home at all, but instead collected his brother and headed for the local pub. Though she had seen little of her husband, in time she grew to enjoy her solitude, the precious time she spent alone with her son, free from Marty's rages and demands.

For a time she had briefly made friends with Jan, who was married to her brother-in-law. Paul was a heavy drinker, as was Marty, and chose to drink his entire weekly recommended level of units in bouts, mostly during the weekend. During the early years of their marriage, Jan had told Bel, she would lie awake waiting for him. When he still wasn't home by four A.M., she would be sweating with fear, worried that something terrible had happened and he was lying dead in a ditch. More recently, she added, that if she had awakened at four A.M. and seen that he was not yet home, she might have *hoped* something terrible *had* happened and he was lying dead in a ditch.

Jan had divorced Paul shortly afterwards. Marty had been deeply enraged on his brother's behalf, and had sternly and angrily warned his wife what would happen if she were ever to try to desert him. But despite his dire warnings, she had left him. Like Jan, she had finally managed to break free.

⚜

Only minutes after the last visitors had left and Gwen had put the "Vacancies" sign in the window, there was a quiet knock at the door. Gwen opened it expectantly, a joyful greeting for her new guests ready on her lips. Her welcoming words died at the sight that met her eyes. The young blonde woman was painfully thin, her reddened eyes half closed against the sun, her face pale and lined, her mouth struggling to return Gwen's smile. The child at her side studied his feet hazily, slightly bemused as though he had just woken up. They had just one small suitcase with them, and the car parked behind them was old and rusty. They were a pitiful sight.

When the young woman spoke, her voice was fragile. "Do you have a room, by chance?"

Hearing the south of England accent, Gwen wondered whether the young mother had been driving all night. As she hurried them both inside Haven's protective walls, Gwen assured them that she had a room that would be just right for the two of them.

"You seem very tired, my dear," she observed when the deposit had been paid and the keys given. "If you'd like to go to your room and rest for a while, Edward and I would be happy to look after your little boy. Our grandchildren are arriving today so we have plenty of toys ready if he'd like to play with them. I'll bring you a bowl of soup in a moment, too, if you'd like."

The woman accepted as though the offer were an oasis in the desert, kissing her son nervously before walking wearily up to her room behind Edward. When Gwen arrived five minutes later with a large bowl of leek and potato soup and a hunk of homemade bread, the woman managed a thin smile and thanked her hungrily. Her face was streaked with tears, Gwen saw, but the color was returning to her cheeks. A good sleep now, followed by a week at Haven, would surely restore her.

CHAPTER 3

J ake Hunt was as delighted to be at Haven as his tired mother was. He had not entirely understood where she was taking him or what exactly they were doing, but he knew that his mother was gentle and smiled tenderly at him whenever he looked to her for reassurance—unlike his father. His father never seemed to be around, especially at bedtime when Jake wanted a story. And when he was home, he never seemed to care what Jake had to show him or to hear what Jake wanted to tell him.

His mother had gently explained that they were going far away and that Daddy wasn't coming, that there would be a new school and new friends for him to play with. This seemed exciting to Jake, especially when, for once, the promise was not one he had to wait and wait for, like a birthday or Christmas. Mum had told him about their adventure as she was putting him in the car and asking him to be as quiet as a mouse, and now here they were. There were wide open spaces for him to run in, lots of exciting new toys, and some nice people who paid him lots of attention.

He went with the Andertons for a lively walk on the mountainside and returned quite tired. Instead of returning to the overflowing box of toys, he settled down with the paper Gwen had left out for him, and began to draw colorful and fantastically shaped people with the new crayons. Edward fetched a refreshing cold drink and a biscuit for his wife and the visiting child, and Gwen settled back into her favorite armchair. She smiled benevolently at the boy, who laughed under her gaze, and commented that her nose and cheeks were all red.

"So are yours," Gwen retorted, adding that the exercise had been good for them. Then she turned her attention to the view of the valley that she never tired of.

She was still reflecting on the joys of children and summer when she heard the throaty chug of a diesel engine, then saw the pale blue Volvo rise up between the trees and pull into the level gravel forecourt. She could not yet see the driver. The afternoon sun was mirrored painfully from the windscreen, but in the back of the car she saw clearly enough some lengths of beveled wood, a fold-up garden chair, and a large stained wooden case, and was curious to know what these might be.

"Is that another arrival?" came the gentle, well-defined voice of her husband, cutting into her thoughts. He had looked up briefly from his newspaper to ask the question but still wore the frown that always covered his face when the lamentable state of the world depressed him.

"I think it's the man who booked your room." She chuckled as she said it for it still amused her that she thought of Room One as Edward's. He had stayed there at least twice a year for many years before their mutual respect and love had been confessed, which in turn led to their recent marriage. She imagined that she might always think of the single room as his.

As Edward folded the paper and put it back onto the table, Gwen stood then bent down to tell the placid child, now prone on the floor and eagerly drawing a sheep of sorts, that they were not going far. The little boy nodded and indicated his latest masterpiece, looking up for their approval. When Gwen and Edward had finished exclaiming over its perfection, they made their way through the door to where their guest was getting out of his car.

He was a man of perhaps fifty, tall and lean with a severe face, deeply etched with lines, startling blue eyes, and thinning hair. He did not smile at them but merely nodded. Taking a small suitcase from the passenger seat, he announced his name briefly without attempting to shake hands.

"Brian McNaught. I have booked." He had a brusque Scottish accent, and there was a questioning note in his voice, as if expecting confirmation of his reservation.

"Yes, indeed, Mr. McNaught. *Croeso i Hafan.* Welcome. I'm Gwen Anderton. This is my husband, Edward. May we help carry your luggage?" She peered again at the mysterious items inside the car.

"No thank you. Just show me to my room. That will be fine." He set off for the door, head lowered, the case in his hand, without waiting to be led or even invited.

Little Jake called out to Gwen as they entered the lounge, so it was Edward who directed the new arrival up the stairs and to the room he had known and loved so well, indicating the bathroom as they passed it. Room One was a small room with the window on the gable end so that it missed the best views. Gwen had compensated for this, however, by buying a plethora of fine watercolor prints by local artists of the best scenery Snowdonia had to offer, and hanging them at regular intervals around the warm peach-colored walls. The room had a handsewn patchwork quilt on the bed, a treasured gift from a missionary couple who had served in Gwen's branch long ago. There was also a deep window sill just the right height to sit on, so Gwen had made a cushion shaped especially to fit. Edward had never been happier than when he was staying in this cosy room, and it brought a lump to his throat to be showing someone else in. He watched Mr. McNaught set the case on the bed and then decided it was perhaps best not to stay and chat.

"Breakfast is at eight o'clock, Mr. McNaught," he said as he began to close the door on the sight of the guest, who was surveying the room with less satisfaction in his features than Edward thought the surroundings deserved.

"I'd like to take it here, if I may," came the quick reply. He did not look up as he spoke.

Edward, a little surprised at the request, tried not to show it. "My wife will bring up a tray."

"I'm hoping for a quiet week. Could you see that I'm not disturbed more than necessary." It was an order, not a question, and those watery blue eyes were still engaged in judging the decor and furnishings. Edward thought it a little rude that Mr. McNaught did not look at him when he spoke.

"We do have some children staying this week. I'll do my best to make sure they're quiet for you," Edward said, then faltered, uncertain of exactly how else Mr. McNaught expected to be disturbed. "Will you be requiring an evening meal tonight?"

"No. Thank you." Mr. McNaught turned his attention to his case. Edward found he was still holding the door handle and the door was half closed, so he pulled it shut, shrugged to himself, and made his way back down the stairs.

Gwen was waiting for him. "Does he like the room?"

Edward sighed and put an arm around her shoulders, a novel action that still thrilled him when he considered how long he had wanted to do it. "I'm sorry, dear. I forgot to ask. I'm still new at this game, I suppose. I almost forgot to ask him about dinner, too. He doesn't want any but he'll take breakfast in his room—except that I forgot to ask what he'd like for breakfast."

"Never mind. I expect he'll be down soon. He's got more things in his car he needs to fetch in. I'll ask him then. It's scripture time, I think, while Jake's busy and before we're disturbed any further."

Edward wondered whether she might be alluding to Angela, for it was early yet, only three-thirty. Nevertheless, he dutifully fetched the books from their shelf and settled beside his wife to read. They read a chapter every day and then discussed it together, sometimes making notes if something seemed particularly important. Gwen was still better at it than he was. She seemed to understand the old language without difficulty, and her knowledge of the scriptures was impressive. She was often able to recall a passage elsewhere that addressed the same topic, and Edward found it difficult not to feel inadequate beside her at times. A member of the Church for less than a year, he had yet to master the workings of the topical guide. Still, he found this time in each other's company to be one of the great joys of married life.

After they had finished reading, they would pray, each offering heartfelt and honest thanks for the other and for their love. Edward hoped that day would never come when they did so by rote. He found that listening to her gentle voice as she read and seeing her glowing face as she looked up at him afterwards, swelled his love for her into something quite spiritual and more than appropriate for prayer.

On this particular day, it was Gwen's turn to offer the prayer. She expressed her love for her new husband and her gratitude for the wise plan for her life, which included him, then went on to ask blessings on their visitors—on Brian McNaught, Belinda Hunt, and Jake (who looked up in surprise at hearing his name), and those yet to arrive. She asked that all enjoy a safe journey, as she always did for her guests, especially, she added guardedly, for Angela and Stuart and their children. Edward was thoughtful as he added his "Amen."

"Are you terribly nervous about seeing them again?" he asked. The stillness after their scripture time was often an excellent time to talk, for the Spirit remained with them for a time and their increased love and warmth for one another helped them to better understand each other's feelings.

"A little," Gwen said, then with some difficulty added, "I don't think your daughter likes me very much."

It hurt him to hear that and knowing that it was true made his stomach knot painfully. He had loved Gwen for many years, but he loved his daughter, too. Gwen had known all about his family long before she had cause to meet them; she had rejoiced with him in the birth of his grandchildren, followed the performance of his son's company on the stock market, and advised him over all the little feuds that were an inevitable part of family life. And yet when she had actually been introduced to them, she had been unprepared for the reality of the other side of his life and for the strong personalities of the children, who took after their father, and who still missed their mother.

Gwen had never been disliked before, he supposed, for who could help but love her kind and easy-going nature, but his children knew nothing of that. They cared only that he wanted to join the strange religion she was involved with, and to marry her and move away from home and from them. They had not hesitated to make their deep suspicion of her obvious, and even though they had refrained from trying to dissuade Edward, in Gwen's presence, from the course he had chosen, they were noticeably absent from his baptism. Angela had stayed only briefly at the wedding, complaining vocally during the friendly reception held afterwards about the lack of alcoholic refreshment and "proper catering."

Gwen had not seen either Angela or Ian since she'd helped Edward pack up his things and move from Birmingham. She had thought it appropriate to invite them to Haven, hoping that a whole week together in this peaceful and beautiful setting might give them a chance to get to know one another. Angela had reluctantly accepted, but Ian had refused her invitation completely.

Seeing Edward's pain, Gwen knew he was wondering if Angela, her husband, Stuart, and the children would arrive today, as they had promised. After all, their arrival would obligate them to attend church tomorrow to hear his talk, and Angela blamed The Church of Jesus Christ of Latter-day Saints for what it had done to her father. Gwen did not like to think about how Angela must be feeling about the Church and now she thought it best that she and Edward speak of other things. She was happier than she had even imagined she might be married to Edward, and in these heady early days, she would not allow anything to intrude on that.

CHAPTER 4

Belinda awoke abruptly with a pounding heart and the shreds of a dream from which she had desperately needed to escape still in her mind. She sat up breathing deeply and took in the charming room about her for a few moments and remembered that she was far away, safe, and that kind people were caring for her little boy downstairs. The pretty curtains could not hide the bright daylight that blazed outside, and checking her watch she saw that she had slept for almost four hours. She was pleased that she had been able to do so.

She was at Haven now, a name that represented safety, security. Remembering that they were staying a whole week, she felt a release as the unknown future crystallized into seven days of tranquility here, beyond which she need not think. The rates were very reasonable and she could afford this little luxury. After all, she had budgeted money for this very purpose. Over three years of secretly saving every penny she could come by had yielded enough to buy herself an old car and to allow for maybe a month of living in a cheap bed and breakfast accommodation, although she hoped it would not take that long before she could support herself and her son.

As she brushed her long hair before going downstairs, she looked at herself in the full-length mirror in her room. She was shocked to see how she had changed in the six years since her wedding day. She had lost the air of trusting innocence so apparent in the wedding photographs; instead there was a fearful resignation in the set of her mouth, the deep line between her eyes, and the way she carried herself. She had assumed a stoop, as though she were ashamed of her height and did not want to be noticed. She still had the fine, long, fair hair that was her best asset, and she dressed well in the long flowing dresses so well suited to her tall frame. However, she was no longer attractively slender but uncomfortably thin, with angular joints and hollowed cheekbones. She stared at herself and saw dead eyes staring back from a pale face.

Seeing herself so changed, she could not help thinking again what she had lost when she had married Marty. Six years ago she had been a bright, articulate girl with a wry sense of humor, just eighteen, a talented dancer and well educated. She had been carefully considering university and planning her career. Then she had met the charming, handsome, and flattering Martin Hunt, ten years her senior. He had showered her with attention and gifts. Six months later had come his dramatic marriage proposal, which quite swept her off her feet with the romance of it all. Overwhelmed at the wondrous prospect of being the first of her friends to marry despite being the shyest, she had accepted, giving up all plans at that point except to live out a life of bliss and security in the arms and cozy home of Marty Hunt.

Had she recognized his shortcomings even then? She could not remember having any serious doubts about marrying him, but perhaps she had forgotten them since, blotted them from her memory so that she did not continually blame herself for her foolishness. How long had it taken her before she had noticed and begun to question why it seemed that her own comfort and happiness meant so little to him?

In the earliest months of their marriage, she had wanted nothing more than to cook and clean. Indeed, to ensure her husband's comfort was a labor of love for the starry-eyed teenager. But not even a year into the marriage, she had begun to learn that it paid to prepare only food that could easily be reheated in the microwave. She had known from the first that he enjoyed nights out at the pub, but then the same was true of her own father. It had not been until his brother, Paul, had moved into an apartment nearby, after his divorce, that Marty had begun to spend night after night in one bar or another, always in Paul's company.

Belinda stretched luxuriously and looked around her room. The room was large, with two firm beds covered with pretty floral eiderdowns. It was simple and clean, and quite adequate, but to Belinda, it was heaven itself. She had stayed in a hotel only once before, on her honeymoon, and her only real memory of that was the sudden stab of bitterness and self-pity as she lay alone late at night, clad in coffee-colored satin and lace, wondering why Marty preferred the hotel bar to being with her. She had fallen asleep long before he had returned to their room, still propped up against the pillows, but had awakened when Marty returned at last, ready for her attentions.

As the months passed, she had felt her dream of happiness slip away and acknowledged to herself that she had simply exchanged her life with her parents—stifling and unfulfilling though it was—for a home filled with tension and cruelty and despair. She was crushed each day by Marty's spiteful drunken words, his criticisms which she came to feel might be warranted, and the blame that always seemed to fall on her. At first she was puzzled by his inconsiderate behavior; time and again she forgave him without being asked. By the time she had realized and accepted the truth about her husband, it was too late; she was pregnant. She knew what kind of man her husband was, but she knew also that her child needed a father, and she still dared hope that fatherhood might change him.

The sleep had refreshed her but now she was hungry once more. She ran the brush though her fine hair, splashed her face with delicious warm water, then hurried downstairs to hug her little boy and thank the Andertons, who had been so kind in entertaining him while she slept.

She ate well that evening, filled with hope for the future. The local lamb with mint sauce was tender and delicious, and Jake even finished all his vegetables without a single word of complaint. Although comfortably full, Bel savored the homemade apple crumble, which melted into the sweet custard in her mouth and was gone too quickly.

Since hers was the only table in the dining room that was occupied, she invited Mr. and Mrs. Anderton to join her, and they chatted about everything and nothing—the weather, the latest bill through

Parliament, and the beautiful view from the window. Mrs. Anderton reported that Jake had enjoyed chasing the sheep during his walk with her that afternoon, and her husband complimented Jake's number skills.

"I was a teacher for many years," he explained. "You've got a very bright lad there."

She glowed at the praise. "He's just turned five so he's due to start school in three weeks." She wondered, as she said it, where this school might be.

"Well, he should do very well there. He's so very sociable and easy-going. A real credit to you, Belinda."

She blushed deeply, unsure of how to accept the compliment. Eventually she just said, "Please, call me Bel." She had asked that of friends and family for years, yet they invariably called her "Lindy."

Gwen smiled. "Well, we hope you'll enjoy your stay, Bel. We'd better get on with the washing up now. Feel free to switch on the television in the lounge if you like." With that, the Andertons excused themselves and carried off the dirty dishes into the kitchen.

Bel sat contentedly at the table for a moment longer, smiling warmly at Jake, who was already beginning to doze in his seat. It really was a new beginning. They had escaped, they were safe at Haven, and she was no longer Marty Hunt's submissive, troubled wife, Lindy.

He stared resolutely into the bottom of his pint glass, as though expecting to find the solution to his problems in the silty dregs there. Seeing his apparent misery, his brother was quick to replace the glass with a full one, but this problem was not one easily fixed with a few drinks. Still, Marty felt comfortable and content here in their usual corner of the Rose and Crown, which was crowded with regulars he knew and where the air was thick with calming smoke and the smell of beer. At some stage, however, he would have to return home, and his house was an empty, lonely place.

It wasn't that he missed his wife exactly. He might have laughed it off if anyone had suggested he loved her, but the truth was, he liked having her around. She was harmless and quiet, she cooked and cleaned for him, and took care of him and his boy. At the memory of Jake, he felt his anger rise again. What right had she to leave like that? Didn't he provide for her? Didn't he take care of her and give her all she needed?

The fresh glass before him was filled with the luminescent amber liquid that promised to help him forget his humiliation. His brother, Paul, sat heavily on the squat bar stool opposite him and licked from his fingers the beer that had overflowed from Marty's glass. Marty took a welcome gulp of the drink and then resumed staring thoughtfully at the table.

"Do you ever think about God?" he said at last.

"No," Paul replied without needing to think about his answer. "Why?"

"I wonder if He's punishing me."

Paul stared at his brother, wondering if he was quite sane. "What for?"

Marty met his eyes and managed a smile. "Good point."

"We'll get her back." Paul was not a man of many words, but his assured tone and squared shoulders showed his determination to see the woman found and punished who had dared to desert his brother.

"How?"

"I'm working on it."

Marty nodded, reassured that his brother would see justice done, whatever it took. Paul could be clever, at least when roused enough by anger to make the effort. Marty drained his glass.

"Another?" he asked Paul.

A group of young women entered the pub, fashionably and scantily dressed, their faces vivid with bold makeup. Their lively chatter and raucous giggles suggested that they were simply here to have a few drinks before moving on to the nightclub down the road. They had caught Marty's eye, and he slicked back his black hair before he swaggered to the bar and joined the throng.

But it just wasn't his night. Despite the charm he knew he still had, and the good looks he shared with his brother, neither of them appeared to interest even the plainest of the girls, and Marty returned to his home at an earlier hour than usual, irritated, dejected, and very drunk. He was growing accustomed to the house being empty when he got back from the pub. Tonight was worse than usual, however, and the rooms felt eerily barren.

He tried the door to Jake's room just to check that she had not changed her mind and returned in his absence. It opened easily. Two beds were cramped into the small room, one of them an uncomfortable old camp bed. Both were unmade and empty. On nights when he was out drinking, Lindy slept in Jake's room, bolting the bedroom door and careful to go to bed long before Marty was due home. He had a bit of a temper when he was drunk, he knew, but he'd only ever hit her on three occasions, and he had always apologized the next morning. It was a bit unreasonable of her to go to such lengths to avoid him, he thought with a scowl.

All the same, whether she was locked away behind this door or in his bed where she belonged, he wanted her back. And he was going to get her back.

CHAPTER 5

By eight-thirty P.M., when Bel and her little boy went up to their room, Angela and her family still had not arrived, nor had the two young men who had booked just yesterday. Mr. McNaught had yet to emerge from Room One, and Gwen, unused to Haven seeming so quiet at this time of year, fretted aloud to her husband. She hoped Mr. McNaught wasn't ill, then she wondered if he wanted a full cooked breakfast in the morning; if she waited any longer to ask, he might already be in bed. Edward looked faintly uneasy at this proposition, knowing of their guest's specific request not to be disturbed. Another time Gwen might have asked what he was thinking, and then yielded to his perceptions, but she wanted a distraction from the thought of Angela's imminent arrival and the animosity that would accompany it.

"What is it?" a voice called several moments after she had knocked on the bedroom door.

"May I come in, Mr. McNaught?" Gwen asked as she did so. Her guest was seated at the window seat, his hands on the seat at his sides. It was a strange position, Gwen thought, but pretended not to notice. She said only, "I wondered whether you'd like a full breakfast or continental in the morning."

"Just some toast, thank you." His smile was forced and his face reddened as he spoke.

Gwen nodded and paused, wondering whether he might be lonely sitting all by himself. "Do you like your room? It is a small one, I know, but—"

"It's fine. But I won't be needing *this*," he said suddenly, cutting her off as though he hadn't heard her. As he spoke, he grabbed the Book of Mormon off the tray where she had left it and thrust it at her, almost throwing it in his eagerness to be rid of it. "I'm not interested in religion," he said curtly. "This sort of thing just clutters the space."

She reached her hand out for the book automatically and tried to laugh off his rudeness. "Oh, it's just a little gift. I always leave a Book of Mormon in the guest rooms. It's a very special volume of scripture—"

He interrupted her again, "Well, I won't be needing it." She thought she detected a slight stammer to his voice before he turned back toward the window, although night had fallen and he could not have been taking in the view. Feeling a little hurt, Gwen turned away and left the room without another word. She had liked every one of her guests in the fifteen years she had been letting rooms at Haven, and as rude as Mr. McNaught appeared, she was determined that he would not be the first one she disliked.

With that encounter behind her, her mind was free again to consider the fact that Angela hadn't yet arrived. The Irish visitors hadn't either, but then, theirs was a long journey, which included a ferry that was often delayed. Angela's only excuse for her lateness was the fact that she didn't actually want to come to Haven, and she especially didn't want to come to church on Sunday.

Gwen's heart sank as she reflected that she had always tried to make Haven a place of love and happiness. But with both Mr. McNaught and Angela to contend with this week, that was going to be extremely difficult.

Belinda was still thinking about Marty as she waited for sleep in her comfortable bed. Even though it was her first night of freedom, her mind was occupied with thoughts of the husband she had left. How had he reacted on discovering she was gone? Would he look for them? Now that she was apart from him, she felt unburdened. She could breathe freely again, as though she were a world away from the cares of her previous life. Nevertheless, the fear that he would find them loomed ominously in the distance.

She knew Marty would not be happy that his son was gone, but there had been no other way. She could not have left Jake behind and she had needed to leave quickly and quietly, without any attempt at explanation, which would have served no purpose at all. That her husband would find her was inevitable, but perhaps not for some time yet. By then, she hoped, she would have gained more strength, perhaps even begun divorce proceedings, and grounded herself firmly somewhere far, far from him.

Hearing a car outside her window, she sat up in bed instantly, all her latent fears crystallized and confirmed. A car easily climbing the steep drive, its engine revving because the driver was showing off, not through necessity. Over the sound of the engine, a loud thumping rhythm emanated from the vehicle, accompanied by no discernible music. The automobile idled for a few moments with a throaty, expectant hum, then abruptly, all sounds from the car were gone, replaced with raised and lively voices.

She found herself somehow at the window and could feel herself trembling as she looked down to the forecourt, mouthing to herself, "No, no, not yet, surely not yet," as though trying to shape reality through the mantra, but as the car doors slammed and the figures moved closer to the farmhouse, a bright automatic light flashed on and she drank in a deep breath again. It was not, as she had feared, her husband and his coarse older brother. She could see only the heads of the young men below, but one was blonde with hair that was just beginning to recede at the temples and the other had dark, close cropped hair. The car was brand new, black, sleek, and shiny with two tail pipes. It could not be further removed from Marty's van or Paul's battered old Ford.

She stayed by the window, at peace now as she listened to her son snoring, and watched as the scene played out below. Obviously in high spirits, the men made no attempt to lower their voices as they hammered on the door, no doubt thinking they had to awaken the occupants in order to gain access.

Both of the Andertons were waiting up for their guests, despite the late hour, and Bel heard Mrs. Anderton greet them with her usual warm welcome. There was not even a hint in the older woman's voice that she was in any way concerned that it was past ten o'clock. The men were even more enthusiastic in their replies, and with lilting Irish accents and a good deal of laughter, they explained that they had become lost trying to find the place. But their apologies were instantly accepted and dismissed by their beaming hosts, and Mr. Anderton walked out to the car to help fetch and carry a suitcase. As the rear door was opened, a dog bounded out, almost knocking him to the ground, and the two men began to laugh.

Bel found that she was laughing, too, and that she felt happy and safe here at Haven. She also felt grateful to the yet unnamed visitors, not only for not being Marty and his brother, but also for demonstrating such youthful vigor and high spirits that even she had felt it.

She awoke to her son's lively smiling face as he shook her shoulders. She kissed the little boy and laughed when he proclaimed that he was starving, even though there was an uncomfortable hollowness in her own stomach.

"Jake darling, I thought I'd never be hungry again after last night's feast, but I'm ready for my fry-up! Must be the mountain air."

As she dressed, she thought about breakfast at home, about how things had been that Friday morning only two days ago. She had awakened first, as usual, and set about the daily task of getting Jake out of bed and then trying to persuade him to get dressed. Once Jake was settled at the table with a bowl of cornflakes, she had taken the sleeping Marty his first cup of coffee of the morning. Eight o'clock sharp, strong and black with two sugars.

She had dressed then as Marty snored. The first coffee always seemed to go cold, but he liked her to bring it all the same, whisper to him that it was there. Sometimes he would wake up enough to watch her dress, his interest fading back into sleep the more clothes she put on.

That Friday she had shaken him awake again, begging money for the shopping. He had opened one eye to look at the shopping list she held, then taken a crumpled twenty-pound note from the wallet at his bedside and dropped it into her outstretched hand. Her eyes had brightened, seeing it. If she was careful and selected the cheaper brands, the items on this list needn't come to more than half that. But Marty would never know. The change from the note would represent a last ten pounds for the escape fund she would be pressing into service that very night.

She persuaded Jake to wash and clean his teeth, then she searched amid the fluff and scraps in Marty's coat pockets for the keys to his van. Hurrying Jake into it, she said something that might have been a prayer as the engine coughed and spluttered. It always started in the end, but that day it had taken several anxious minutes.

Early morning was the best time to shop at the discount supermarket, she had found, when there were still a few of the cheapest economy loaves on the shelves, and yesterday's surplus stock was heavily discounted. Eggs, milk, bread, cheese, potatoes, some apples for Jake, and Marty's cigarettes. Her careful selection resulted in the expected ten pounds in change. Every little bit helped.

Once the shopping was put away, it was time for Marty's second cup of coffee, only one sugar this time, and brown toast with thick-shred marmalade. He was usually awake by this time, although on that Friday she had been halfway through the ironing before she had heard the floorboards creak as his feet finally met the carpet.

He had left for his building job on the other side of town—installing a kitchen—just before the child she tended arrived. At the split-second timing, she had heaved a sigh of relief, as Marty did not know about her two-day-a-week childminding. If he did, he might wonder what she was doing with the money she earned and why she needed it.

Thinking back to last Friday, she realized that she never seemed to eat breakfast at home. Her morning routine was so automatic and so based around the comfort of her husband, son, and young charge, that it was only now that she realized why she always found herself so hungry looking at the freshly baked bread on the supermarket shelves. She could almost smell it now, floury and crisp and soft as cotton-wool inside . . . but it was the smell of bacon and sausages, which reminded her she was actually at a cozy and comfortable bed and breakfast, and she was about to tuck into a really good, full English breakfast. Or rather, a good, full *Welsh* breakfast, she reminded herself, and she was going to enjoy it thoroughly.

CHAPTER 6

The dining room, now flooded with morning light, was as charming as the rest of the ancient farmhouse. It had dark, broad oak beams across the ceiling and tiny, deep-set leaded windows, which offered tantalizing glimpses of the beautiful sunny valley. The walls that were not exposed stone were plastered and painted white. Sparkling white linen, and crockery set alongside bright flowers from the garden, adorned the four round tables about which sat a less aesthetic assortment of visitors.

Bel cast a look around and recognized the two men who had arrived late the previous night. They were around her own age, she judged, both tall and lean, casually dressed and wearing relaxed smiles, their faces occasionally erupting into natural laughter whenever their already spirited conversation reached an amusing point. Both had brown eyes although the blond young man hid his under long lashes, which completed a strongly set and pleasing face. His dark-haired companion had a Roman slant to his nose and large, hooded eyes that gave him a slightly aristocratic appearance seemingly at odds with his more animated personality.

The other group, a young family, was one she had not seen. She wondered where they had been at dinner or if they had arrived even later than the young men had. The parents were in their early thirties perhaps, but the three children very young. They had a boy of around

Jake's age, another boy of about two, who was staring at his plastic fork from a high chair, and a baby whose age was surely still counted in weeks cradled in a bouncing seat set on the floor beside his mother. The woman seemed strangely familiar although Bel was certain she had never seen her before. Her short bright red hair was cut into a severe and angular but easy-care style and was the only remarkable thing about her, for she was of average height and build with no notable features except the expression on her face. It was one of controlled anger, firmly set into the straight line that was her mouth, as immovable as though she had been born furious. Her husband sported equally unusual hair, a mass of blonde curls, but his worn, tired face bore an expression of resigned acquiescence.

The fourth table had only one place setting and was empty. A late sleeper, Bel thought, and checked her watch. As if on cue Mr. and Mrs. Anderton burst through the door from the kitchen carrying trays, which in turn bore plates filled to the very edges with fried eggs, bacon and sausages, mushrooms, baked beans, grilled tomatoes, and fried bread, which tasted as wonderful as it smelt. There was crisp toast to mop up the grease and yet more slices to smother with home-made jams and marmalade, and steaming pots of tea to wash it all down. Perfect, Bel sighed happily. A full stomach made contentment that much easier to come by.

The wonderful Andertons appeared again some time later to clear the tables, looking quite content themselves, and as Mr. Anderton piled up the trays again, Mrs. Anderton rapped on the empty table for attention.

"I do hope you've all enjoyed your breakfasts. Now, since my husband and I are members of The Church of Jesus Christ of Latter-day Saints and this is the Sabbath day, we will be going to church this morning. I know in most guest houses there would be a Sunday lunch instead of evening meal, but since we won't be back until two P.M., we will have dinner at six o'clock as usual. We have space in our car and we'd like to invite any of you who would like come along to join us. The branch meets at Nefyn, and it takes almost an hour to get there, so we will be leaving in about thirty minutes. Just let us know; we'd be more than happy to have you along, particularly since my husband is giving a talk today."

Bel thought she heard a tremor in Mrs. Anderton's voice and noticed that the last sentence seemed to be directed toward the family seated at the next table. The young mother was looking down at her knife and shaking her head in something akin to disbelief. Bel watched this strange reaction in puzzlement, and as she turned her attention back to her toast her eyes caught those of the dark young man who sat opposite her. He had also apparently noticed the pointedness of the words and had looked toward the family, frowning slightly. Bel smiled at him and he smiled and shrugged in reply, as if they both shared the same question: what was so important about the red-haired woman attending church?

＊＊＊＊＊＊＊

Gwen knew as soon as she saw Angela's reaction that she was offended to be asked. But, she reasoned, she always invited the guests to church and was not about to stop just because she had already argued with her daughter-in-law on the matter.

The proprietress of Haven had been slightly irritated, although she tried not to be, that Angela's family had arrived so late—almost eleven P.M. Edward's daughter had given Gwen the unconvincing excuse that the children could fall asleep in the car and just be transferred to their cots when they arrived. The children had indeed slept on the journey as young children always did, but had then awakened bright and happy once at Haven and had refused to settle down again.

Gwen knew that Angela had accepted that as a calculated risk; it gave her another reason to politely say that she was too tired to come to church. All the same, Gwen was honest by nature and would almost have preferred that Angela admit they had deliberately come late because they didn't really want to be at Haven at all, and they would not be coming to hear Edward's talk that morning because they objected to Gwen's church on principle.

Still thinking about her new daughter-in-law as she climbed the stairs to collect Mr. McNaught's tray, Gwen had quite forgotten that Mr. McNaught had also been less than cordial the previous day. She knocked smartly and went in when he called. The visitor was in the process of putting on his coat, and she was pleased to see that he had eaten all his breakfast, what little it was. As she picked up the tray, she wished him good morning for the first time—since Edward had taken the tray up earlier—then extended to him the same invitation to church as she had the guests in the dining room.

"As I told you yesterday, I'm not interested in religion." He glared at her.

She could do nothing but stare back, lost for words until she managed to explain with an unintentionally apologetic tone to her voice, "I always invite my guests to church with me." She could think of nothing more that might appease him or convey to him that she meant no affront to his opinions and was just extending a courtesy.

"Well, it's inappropriate," he grumbled. "I came here for some peace and quiet. I didn't expect anyone foisting their beliefs on me."

"I'm sorry," she stammered, wondering even as she did so what she had to apologize for.

"I'll be going out now and I won't be back until this evening. I'd like dinner in my room tonight please." He almost knocked the tray out of her hands as he swept hurriedly past her and down the stairs.

Edward saw Mr. McNaught's hasty exit, heard him start his car, and speed off down the steep driveway faster than was safe. This was followed by Gwen's pale face and red eyes as she stepped carefully down the stairs, the cup on the tray she carried rattling on its saucer as her hands trembled. Edward was as intelligent and observant as his wife and could easily guess what had happened and what needed to be done. He bade her put the tray down and then wrapped his arms around her and held her close to him as she gulped back tears. They said nothing for some moments, for nothing needed to be explained, until Gwen looked up at her dear husband and said, "I am *so glad* I've got you!"

⁂

Stuart Kirby, irritated by his wife's stoniness and more than a little tired of the grudge that had so disrupted their hitherto placid existence, decided at breakfast that the time had come for him to put an end to it once and for all. He was quite determined to find something about Gwen Anderton that Angela might relate to, sympathize with, even like. This one-sided feud was becoming tedious, and while he had never been the most sensitive of men when it came to complex interpersonal relationships, he knew he had to set aside his ineptness and inexperience and do something to restore the peace. There was nothing else for it. Angela was stuck with Gwen as a stepmother, and she had better start getting used to it. After all, it wasn't as though she had to live in Gwen's home forever or even see her all that often.

As he searched for something that might soften his wife towards her, his eyes fell upon the thick slice of bacon in much the same instant his knife did, and he wondered whether the way to Angela's heart might not be through her stomach. He chewed thoughtfully on the succulent salty sliver and swallowed it with a gulp so that he could say his piece to his wife, practically the first words they'd spoken since the sight of Gwen in the dining room had sent her into that foul mood again.

"I'll say one thing for her, she's an excellent cook. This breakfast is quite delicious." He had hoped that she might respond with the dignity of a reply, but the snort she gave was quite the opposite. He had been certain that she, too, was enjoying her meal, but now it seemed suddenly to have turned to poison in her mouth. She chewed as though in the late stages of tetanus and pushed her knife and fork together when her plate was still half full. It was another minute before she spoke again.

"Cut Adam some more toast, will you, Stuart?"

He obeyed, glad that his young son was enjoying the meal at least. As he chatted with his small son, using the few words Adam knew, Stuart found it nevertheless more stimulating conversation than his wife could offer in her present state. She was pointedly stirring the tea, her spoon clinking noisily against the edges of the teapot as she pushed the bedraggled teabag around and around in the tepid water, as though trying to wash it clean. Stuart knew Mormons didn't drink tea and he wondered if his wife might be trying to make the point that she liked it, lots and lots of strong, evil tea. It was a bit silly of her, he thought, since Gwen wasn't even in the room to notice, but perhaps Angela was doing it for her own reasons. Judging from the face she pulled as she drank it, she no doubt felt they were good ones.

When every last drop was gone from Angela's china cup, Stuart released Adam from the high chair, and Angela scooped up Rosie without a word. Then, with a nod to the other guests, they walked back to the lounge. Stuart was still wondering what else he might say to help Angela see Gwen's good side when he realized with a sudden shock that the answer was nothing. In the center of the room stood Angela's father and his bride, locked in an embrace that Stuart thought looked rather sweet. Edward was stroking Gwen's hair while whispering words of comfort, and Stuart could feel his wife beside him stiffen as she grew even more pale and her eyes flashed with renewed rage.

"Dad! How could you?" she spat.

Unruffled, Edward nevertheless released Gwen from his arms slowly and reluctantly, checking as he did so that his wife was feeling better. Then, turning his attention to his daughter, he asked mildly, "How could I what?"

"At your age! And in public!"

He raised an eyebrow. "Angela, old and decrepit though I may be, I am still entitled to hug my wife and certainly in our own home."

The younger woman glared at Gwen, as though hoping her gaze might cause her father's new wife to melt in shame. Knowing that Gwen was not feeling her best that morning, Edward whispered to her to keep quiet and leave this to him. But Angela continued, "Your *wife* is turning in her grave to see you carrying on with this woman. It's a good thing you have children to keep her memory alive."

Seeing that the other guests were starting to come out of the dining room, Edward decided that now was not the time or place for this conversation. "We're going to church now, Angela. We'd love you to come. I'm giving a talk today, and it would mean a lot to me."

His daughter declined with a selection of words which had never been spoken at Haven before and which were heard by the other guests as they left the dining room. Edward was intensely ashamed of her but pleased when Stuart cut in quickly and, for him, surprisingly well.

"Rosie needs changing, Angela. Let's take the kids upstairs and sort them out."

The mood lightened considerably after that, and as Gwen put on her coat, she chatted with the other guests, acting as if nothing particularly unusual had occurred. Only Edward saw that her smile was a trifle strained and that her lips trembled. Putting a gentle arm around her, he led her out the door and helped her into the car before they set out on the long drive to church.

CHAPTER 7

Edward was ashamed to find himself shaking with nerves as he sat beside his wife in the small rented hall in Nefyn waiting for sacrament meeting to begin. This was his third talk in his first year as a member of the Church, and even as he prayed for confidence and inspiration, he despaired of ever speaking with the naturalness and ease of some of the missionaries and long-time members. He had struggled through the topical guide and Gwen's collection of books and magazines to prepare, and knew that standing before the congregation, he would have to battle with the thin pages of his still unfamiliar scriptures as he flipped backwards and forwards, trying to find the references he had written on his notes.

Earlier he had expressed his dissatisfaction with his own abilities to his wife, and in her wonderfully reassuring and loving way, she had told him that he did not have to deliver a sermon fit for the general conference of the Church, and for its eleven million members throughout the world. He need only give the best he could of himself and in this manner serve his small branch and its members. The smallest, simplest messages might give strength, and the good example of one willing to deliver them always did.

All the same, even though he had gained a testimony of the gospel—surprised at the ease by which it came once he had finally ventured to seek the truth—he still felt new. He had a calling of sorts as first counselor to the Young Men, of whom there were only three in the branch, and his marriage to Gwen had ensured his immediate acceptance into the hearts of those who knew her. He was lucky to have Gwen to answer all the questions he still had about how something was pronounced, or whether an activity was appropriate on the Sabbath, or whether it was permitted to ask the missionaries their first names, but he felt foolish each time for needing to ask. When a teenager had followed him into the waters of baptism two months after his own baptism, he had been pleased not to be the newest member of the branch any more. Even so, not being the newest did not make him any less new.

There were two sister missionaries in the branch now, and that had been something else new. He had only known elders or couples before. Sister Morrison was Australian, tall and slender with a happy earnestness about her and fair hair that she always tied back. Her companion, Sister Keene, was from Idaho, petite, dark, bespectacled, and confident as she swished about in her smart ankle-length skirts. He liked the sisters but meeting them had led to a rash of new questions. Why were sister missionaries older than elders? Why did they serve shorter missions? Why were there fewer of them? A lifelong Anglican by birth and habit, rather than conviction, he sometimes still longed for the comfort of sitting on a hard pew in a well-known church, where he knew every syllable of the service by heart and understood every nuance and tradition—in fact, knew everything about it except whether it was really *true*. Here he knew the truth of the gospel preached to him, but seemingly so very little else.

He delivered his talk with his voice and hands still shaking, his scriptures still near-pristine despite the frantic thumbing he subjected them to each time he gave a talk. He had a sinking feeling in his heart that he was not telling these precious people anything they had not heard before. But his audience was uncomplaining and patient, and except for the smallest children, each member appeared to hang on his every word. Nevertheless, he could not shake the feeling that he was not really imparting anything new or inspiring. He realized that every well-known and well-loved person who looked steadily at him as he spoke knew more about the gospel and scriptures than he did, and wondered whether he could really teach them anything.

When he sat down afterwards, Gwen squeezed his hand and then, sensing more was needed, kissed his cheek. Not realizing that this might be appropriate in church, he reddened, remembering, as he so often seemed to, the time he had applauded the Primary sacrament meeting presentation in a loud, embarrassing solo.

Today was a particularly bad day to give a talk, since he was also nervous about the interview immediately following the meetings. When the time came, he meekly and quietly followed President Chugg into the small vestibule that served as an office. Edward liked the branch president very much. He and his wife were missionaries from Washington state, and they had such an honest warmth about them that Edward had loved them from the moment they arrived to replace President and Sister Burton. President Chugg was wearing his habitual wide smile as he placed a friendly hand on Edward's shoulder in an attempt to put him at ease.

"Brother Anderton, that was a wonderful talk you gave. Thank you." To President Chugg, everything was "wonderful," and yet it was impossible to doubt that he really was delighted by everything around him.

"Do you think so? I was worried it was a little shallow, that I had nothing new to say," Edward said humbly.

"Not at all. You have such a fresh understanding of the scriptures, it is a joy to listen to you," the president reassured him.

It was all he needed to hear, and Edward smiled. A well-educated man, he was fairly confident in his learning and ability, his only failure perhaps being his intense desire to please which, in his last marriage, had resulted in him being little more than a servant to his demanding wife. He might have been in his element in this church where service was such a respected and revered occupation except that, as yet, a true opportunity to serve had not yet arisen. Mindful of his newness and his age, the priesthood leaders of the branch had been careful with the burdens they had placed upon him, and up until now his greatest challenge had been the talk he had just given.

The one-year anniversary of his baptism would be in just two weeks' time, however, and in the months since that wonderful day he had demonstrated again and again his eagerness to learn, his faithfulness, and his studiousness and intelligence. Edward felt this interview would be the greatest test he would ever face as a member of the Church, but wise leaders of the Church, such as President Chugg, knew that the future for dependable Latter-day Saints such as Edward was filled with opportunity and promised blessings.

President Chugg spoke slowly and with clarity. "You will soon have been a member of the Church for a year. I know that you and Sister Anderton have been planning a visit to Salt Lake City for your temple sealing. She has friends there, I believe?"

Edward nodded solemnly.

"First of all, I want to make it quite clear to you that this temple recommend interview is not a mere formality. The ordinances and endowments that will precede the sealing ceremony are not just matters to be 'got through.' So, if you have any doubts or concerns whatsoever, you should tell me now, even if it means upsetting your travel plans and disappointing your wife. These matters are too important to be trifled with."

President Chugg proceeded to ask several questions relating to Edward's obedience to gospel principles and practices, and Edward listened closely to each question. Then, after he had thoroughly considered each question, he answered as honestly and carefully as he could, fearful that if he got it wrong here, then what would follow in that special, wonderful temple might not be valid. It all had to be right and perfect; he had to know what he was doing. He felt a renewed appreciation for the preparatory classes he had taken, even though with only two in the class it had been a quiet and strained process, and also for the many books he had read and the advice Gwen had given him. He was ready, he felt, or at least as ready as he could be when he still felt so new.

When the formal questions were over and President Chugg asked if there was anything else he might need to discuss, Edward spoke of his concerns that he still had so much to learn and was surprised when the older man laughed.

"That feeling never goes away," he said, still chuckling. "I still want to ask questions and then worry that I'll look stupid. We work with so many converts and see them go so far and change in such wonderful ways that only a few weeks ago I asked Sister Chugg whether she thought a convert would ever become President of the

Church. You know what she said? 'I think you'll find that a few already have.' Think about it." He smiled at Edward as he sat back in his chair before continuing.

"In fact, I just learned something new myself," he confided. "I asked the stake president how it was that you and Gwen were planning to be sealed in the temple only four months after your civil marriage. In the States, you see, when a couple choose to marry outside the temple, there is a one-year waiting period before they can be sealed in the temple. But President Donaldson explained to me that in Britain, temple marriages are not legally recognized, so a couple must undergo a civil ceremony before they are sealed, so there is no such restriction here." Edward smiled at his branch president, grateful for the man's honesty and good humor. It was a relief to know that even this lifelong member whom he admired so much still didn't know all there was to know about the gospel and the workings of the Church.

President Chugg smiled conspiratorially. "It may be a bit early yet to speak of this, but I happen to know that when Sister Chugg and I go home, there are no plans to send any more couples to serve in the Nefyn branch."

Edward had read in a recent *Ensign* that there was a shortage of couple missionaries. "Oh really?" he said questioningly, fully expecting that to be the reason.

"Oh yes. The branch has grown so much in the last year, it's stronger now than ever. The mission and stake presidency feel that it's time the branch president was chosen from among one of the members. The reason I am telling you this, Brother Anderton, is so that you can understand fully that in this church, it is the members who hold the callings, not just those of us who have chosen to serve missions. You have made a sacred covenant in being baptized and you will soon be making more. I feel that if you remain faithful, then, with your talent for understanding and conveying the gospel so well, you may well be called to leadership positions in the Church yourself one day. You will probably not feel worthy or qualified, but Heavenly Father calls whom He chooses in His wisdom."

Edward stared in astonishment as the branch president signed the thin slip of paper, then placed it before him. What President Chugg was saying was that he, Edward Anderton, member of less than one year, could very well be called to a leadership position. It might even be possible that he would be called to serve as the branch president! The only branch presidents or bishops he had met so far had been lifelong members, and he respected and honored them all. He had never imagined that he might serve in a branch presidency himself. At a complete loss for words, he looked at the paper in front of him with its beautiful gold image of the temple before picking up the pen and carefully signing it. He felt that he had "arrived" at last.

CHAPTER 8

F unny business that," Steven Collins said to his friend Danny, sitting back in the armchair and wondering if there was a Sunday paper. Steve had witnessed only the last few words of the confrontation, but that had been enough to pique his interest.

Danny O'Hanlon was only half listening, his eyes roving across the spines of the books on the shelves before him. "Must be part of the family," he mumbled, absorbed in his search.

Steve looked intrigued at his friend's insight. "What makes you say that?"

"You only get that type of feud in a family," Danny explained, with a quick look at Steve. "They're not just residents who didn't like their breakfast, are they? You'd never see that sort of blowup from strangers who only arrived yesterday." Finding a book that interested him, Danny flipped it off the shelf.

"What are you reading?" Steve asked after a minute, having concluded that there was no Sunday paper and hoping there might be something as light, entertaining, and devoid of current events elsewhere.

"*Women and Property in the Early Twentieth Century,*" Danny replied, tut-tutting over the injustice of what he was reading and not entirely concentrating on what Steve was saying.

Steve was bored already, and they had arrived only a few hours ago. He was debating how he might regain his friend's attention, short of shouting at him, when the woman from the next table walked in with the mischievous-looking little boy. Now there was something that might pull Danny out of his book. The young mother was slim and blonde and passable, and a child didn't necessarily mean she was spoken for. She was there alone, wasn't she? Now, how to get her talking? Steve studied her, wondering. He almost never had trouble talking to women; he knew he could be quite appealing when he made the effort.

"Excuse me. Did Mr. and Mrs. Anderton mention anything about a Sunday paper to you before they left?"

Without a word, the woman shrugged and shook her head.

"If you want to know the day's news," Danny said, still standing at the bookcase, intent on his book, "why don't you turn the television on?"

"Because I don't want the news," his friend replied. "I want the crossword."

"Surely there'll be one in yesterday's paper?" the woman ventured timidly.

Although Steve acknowledged that could well be the case, he paid no attention to the older newspapers on the table. He preferred to talk to a pretty lady, even if she did have a child.

"Join us for a minute?" he invited her. "It's always a bit dull when Danny gets his nose stuck in a book. It would be nice to have some company. I'm Steve and that's Danny."

Her son appeared bright for a five-year-old, but he had no particular desire to engage in boring grown-up discussions about the weather, so he turned his attention to the box of toys again. Danny even put down his book and sat beside her.

Steve explained that they had come all the way from Waterford, in the Republic of Ireland, hoping for a week's sunshine so they could do some rock climbing and canoeing. They had exhausted all the interesting climbs and rivers within easy reach of home.

"What about you? Where are you from?" he asked the taciturn woman, who hesitated.

"South," she said simply.

He waited and when she said no more, he asked what had brought her to Haven.

She shrugged. "It seemed nice."

Steve and Danny exchanged glances, intrigued by this mysterious woman. "Are you going to tell us your name, since we've told you ours," Steve asked, "or do we just call you Madam Mystery?"

"Bel," she replied simply, then as if fearful that they were prying too much, she began to ask them questions. "So what do you two do for a living? And where was that again?"

"We work in a big hotel together," Steve said. "In Waterford. Danny's a waiter and I'm a chef."

Bel nodded, then was silent.

Now it was Danny who began to question Bel. "What did you think of the invitation this morning?" He leaned toward her and laughed a little when she jumped, startled at his nearness.

"To go to church with our host and hostess?" Bel asked. "I was a little surprised, but I think the Andertons meant well. I know Mormons have a reputation for aggressive proselytizing, but these people just wanted to be polite and share something with us that means a lot to them."

"We did consider going," Danny admitted. "We were thinking it might be a laugh, but then I felt it wasn't right, that we were only going for the sake of a bit of entertainment. It wouldn't be fair on Mr. and Mrs. Anderton that we weren't taking it seriously."

"Do you have any religious beliefs of your own?" Bel asked tentatively.

Danny's face was thoughtful as he considered her question. "I come from a Catholic family. My folks don't go to church and didn't bring me up in it, but I believe in God. I always have. There are so many conflicting teachings about who He is and what He wants of us that it would take me a good few years to sort through them and make a firm decision what I want to do about His existence. To be honest—" he gave a shrug and laughed, "— I'm just too young at the moment to want to worry about all that just now."

She nodded in understanding. "How old are you?"

"Twenty-four. Steve there says religion has caused all the wars and conflicts and evil in the world, but I've studied some history in my spare time. While that might be partly true, religion has also shaped our world, driven it, progressed it. It's been the force behind some really important people and achievements. The English novel, the printing press, the abolition of slavery—all came about because someone had deep religious beliefs. Then, of course, there are the moral absolutes it provides, and it's difficult to know where else we would have come up with those. No, if it weren't for religion, I think our world would be one of anarchy and apathy, so I have a great deal of respect for Mr. and Mrs. Anderton for knowing what they believe and why and having the courage to say so."

Bel was quite awed by this speech. She agreed entirely with this, feeling that this young man had just said exactly what she had thought for years, albeit more eloquently than she could ever have phrased it. Steve seemed less impressed, however, and even a little put out for some reason.

"Now how can you say all that and then laugh at my beliefs?" he said, pouting just a little.

"Your beliefs aren't any sort of religion," Danny scoffed. "They're just superstition. There's a big difference."

"What beliefs are those?" Bel asked, interested.

Steve's voice was very serious as he spoke. "I study astrology. I know a woman who has a remarkable gift for second sight, and I visit her quite regularly for guidance."

"It's a load of rubbish," Danny said, though there was no spite in his voice. "She's never told you anything that she couldn't have guessed by looking at you or didn't have an odds-on chance of being right about."

It was soon obvious to Bel that this was a long-standing debate between the two young men. "How can you believe in God, which is one type of supernatural thing, and not in astrology?" Steve demanded. "What's the difference?"

Danny sighed and then explained patiently, "Because all reason and logic points to there being a great mind and purpose behind the complexity of the universe, but there is no sense at all in the proposition that the movements of great planets millions of miles away can affect our little insignificant lives."

"Their gravitational fields—" Steve began defensively, but his friend cut in.

"They are much too far away for their gravity to have any effect on us at all. You'd have to be in orbit around a planet before you even had to start thinking about gravity." Danny flashed a quick grin at his friend that took in their new acquaintance as well. "Of course, I can't help what planet you are personally in orbit around."

As Bel felt her lips curving into a helpless smile at these two young men and their comfortable banter, there was a sudden commotion beneath the small coffee table. She heard the thumping of a wagging tail on wood, and then found herself face to face with two searching brown eyes that shone warmly with the faithfulness of a Labrador. The dog studied her for a moment, then raised its front paws onto her lap and proceeded to lick her face. Bel laughed and pushed it away as Jake rushed over, perhaps thinking he might persuade the dog to play with him.

"Someone's woken up at last. She's a lazy old thing on a Sunday morning," Steve said.

"What's the dog called?" Bel asked Danny as she scratched the animal's floppy ears and accepted more sloppy affection.

Danny smiled gently and it was clear that he loved the dog. "Lucy. She's the stupidest animal on the planet, chews everything. She's Steve's dog and he never goes anywhere without her. He nearly got sacked once for bringing her into the kitchen at work, so now she guards the cold storage shed while he's working. Eats well most nights, too."

Bel laughed, imagining the exotic scraps that must find their way to the Labrador. She was starting to relax, she discovered with some surprise. She might even have said she was happy. Danny was easy to talk to, pleasant, and open, and she liked him. He spoke with a careless confidence and even his posture exuded self-assurance. She saw something else too, something suggested by his quick answers, and by the hint of underlying boredom in the way he looked around himself or read books as he carried on a conversation. She saw in him a swift, analytical mind starved of stimulation, and she wondered how it was that he was only a waiter at a hotel instead of a promising student or high-flying businessman.

She was only twenty-four herself, but she had the unexpected thought that these two lads were still quite immature. It was unlikely that they had experienced much of the trials and sorrows of life or shouldered any responsibility to speak of. She thought Danny, in particular, was more interested in having fun and taking it easy, as if he didn't care to exert himself or apply his intellect toward the benefit of his life, future, and career. Bel realized they were the same age, and yet she had a five-year-old child she was responsible for. She had even gone hungry so that the bills could be paid and her son clothed and fed while her husband had thought nothing of spending half his pay at the pub in a single weekend.

These boys, she imagined, probably lived at home with their hardworking fathers and adoring mothers, spending their pay on clothes, vacations, and nights out, with never a thought to the future. But there was no contempt in her as she considered their immaturity. If not for Jake, she would have given anything to change places with them.

Danny was speaking and she realized she hadn't been listening. He repeated the question. "I said, have you got any plans for this afternoon?"

She shook her head. "Not really. I thought we'd just relax for today, maybe take a walk or something. I'll be traveling a bit further afield tomorrow." *When the job centers open,* she might have said but did not. Today she would take stock, recover from the last six years, and prepare for what lay ahead. Perhaps she should have accepted the invitation to church with Mr. and Mrs. Anderton, she thought, frowning a little. It might have given her some peace and strength.

"We were thinking of going to Criccieth to see the castle. Care to join us?"

Bel wondered that Danny could invite them with such confidence without first checking with his friend. They must have known each other well for many years. As Danny had surely guessed, Steve seemed quite at ease with the proposal. "Great idea. Come along, the more the merrier. In fact, why don't we stop somewhere for lunch together on the way?"

"No, I—I couldn't." She looked away. "Come on, Jake. Time to brush your teeth."

Danny was having none of it. "Go on, it'll be fun. We'd really like to have you come along, both of you."

She liked these young men, and despite herself she trusted them. It would be good to spend time with them, she decided. Given her experience with men thus far in her life, she might never trust another, but although she had known these two only a few minutes, they seemed open and genuine and fun. Finally she accepted with thanks, wondering what she was getting herself into.

She sat back after the young men had gone up to their room, looking forward to that afternoon with a strange contentment she could not remember ever feeling before. Less than two days free and already she was happy, Jake was enjoying himself, she had made friends, and the Andertons were kind and thoughtful. What a miraculous place this was.

CHAPTER 9

When Bel had set out in the early hours of that Saturday morning, she had not really known where she was heading. She was just following the motorways northward, trying to put as much distance between herself and her past as possible. It had been a whim that had brought her into Wales, a notion that the actual crossing of a border into another country— although still part of the United Kingdom—symbolized in some way the leaving behind of all that she wanted to forget. She had never been to Wales before, although she had long wanted to, which was something of a problem for her now. Whereas most holiday-makers might have some idea of the sights and attractions of the area they are visiting before they arrived, Bel would have been hard put to even roughly pinpoint their location on a map. She had no idea of what to expect from Criccieth, or even how long it might take to get there. Was the castle a ruin or inhabited, and were they visiting a large city, where there would be good shopping, a Sunday market, or car boot sale? Or would it be only a hamlet, boasting of little else beyond a few ancient castle walls?

Sitting in the backseat of Steve's car, Bel took Jake's hand in hers. Steve was driving, and Danny sat up front with him. Bel always got carsick traveling in the backseat of cars, and within thirty minutes of leaving Haven, was starting to feel more than a little queasy, due in no small part to Steve's manic driving. He hurtled round the bends of the narrow road and almost stood on the accelerator during the straights while Danny sat nonchalantly beside him, unperturbed by a couple of near misses. Bel could not decide whether Steve always drove like this or whether both were simply showing off—Steve his driving prowess and Danny his nerves of steel.

Jake sat bolt upright beside his mother, trying to appear manly even though he was deathly pale. The music that both men loved blared out as loud as ever and animated the two young men, who squirmed rhythmically in their bucket seats. It seemed tuneless to Bel, whose tastes were more classical, but she found Danny's complete lack of self-consciousness as he sang amusing.

When at last the car flew around another bend and the vista of Criccieth opened up before them, Bel was both relieved and delighted. The small town hugged the gently rounded shoreline of a wide bay, across which, in the far distance, she could see the mountains. Dominating the skyline and rising out of the sea was a huge mound, upon which stood the castle, its twin towers and half-ruined but imposing walls overlooking the town and the bay. It was a beautiful aspect, and the appearance of the sign for Criccieth—on which one of the middle "c's" had been blotted out by nationalist vandals—gave Bel new heart to fight the waves of nausea rising up in her as large as any of the breakers on the beach.

The road continued into the high street where there were a few shops and a large and imposing but grimy structure fronting the street in its center. Faded lettering on its gabled wall declared it to be a hotel.

"Lunch here?" Steve suggested, seeing the sign outside offering three-course Sunday lunches. There was general agreement, and he braked sharply at the same time as he pulled the car in toward the curb to park.

The hotel had a strange air of faded glory, for its wood-paneled walls and grand winding staircase were obviously once the ultimate in luxury. But now its carpets were wearing thin, its decor was out of date, and its furnishings were old and worn. In the large dining room the servers handed them menus that were so old that the ink was now indelibly transferred to their torn plastic coverings, spelling mistakes and all. As Bel and the others made their selection from the limited choice of starters and main courses, all plain roast meats with vegetables, a radio played the latest hits. Service was quick, it was evidently all ready prepared, and the food was palatable if bland. From where they were seated close to a window, they could look out on Steve's car only a few feet away and see Lucy staring sadly back at them with her large brown eyes.

It had been impossible to talk properly in the car with the intermittent roaring of the engine and continuous blaring of the music, but they chatted easily here. Bel was starting to feel more comfortable with these Irish lads and began to ask them the usual questions about their background and lives, carefully fielding those same questions, however, when they were directed back to her.

"We're not really supposed to be here," Steve said with a wicked grin.

"What do you mean?"

"We're not allowed to take holiday from work between June and September. It's the busiest time, you know. But it's been a tough summer and we're only halfway through it, so we decided we needed to recharge the batteries a bit . . ."

"We told the rest of the staff," Danny added, "to make sure they could cope without us and, er, failed to turn up on Saturday morning." He and Steve laughed, wondering aloud if they would even have jobs to go back to, an attitude Bel found hard to understand.

But Jake seemed to like the lads and he loved their dog, Lucy. Over dinner he discovered that both he and Danny liked the same computer game, so the entire dessert course was spent listening to a debate between Danny and the five-year-old about whether one needed the knife and the ruby to get to Level Four. Although she hadn't a clue what they were talking about, Bel was happy to hear them and listened with contentment. She liked Danny, and for some reason, it was important to her that Jake did, too.

They left the car where it was and walked to the castle just ten minutes away, Lucy bounding beside them and straining at her leash. Bel bought a guidebook, reading about the castle's history with great interest and discovering that the original part of the castle was almost a thousand years old. The four visitors made the steep ascent to the top of the mound and stood alongside the ruined walls. Bel was captivated by the view, which stretched for miles, with the sea on three sides and another, larger castle visible across the bay. Turning around, she could see all of Criccieth, from the small school to the hotel where they had just eaten lunch.

Danny and Steve did not even bother to read the plaques about the purpose of each section of the castle. They particularly failed to notice the ones requesting visitors not to climb on the walls, for no sooner had they walked into the large grassy courtyard than they were climbing up the ruins, finding footholds and handholds easily in the large rocks. Bel worried that Jake would try to follow, but he seemed to know his limits.

Some of the ancient stone steps remained, which made it easy for him to get to the top of one of the lower broad walls and walk along it. Danny and Steve gallantly applauded him from their positions at the top of the towers. They had raced each other and now each hugged a flagpole as they waved at Bel fifty feet below. Bel was pleased she hadn't watched them climb up for she would have been frightened for them. She told Danny so when he was safely back on the ground, adding that as an experienced climber he surely knew how important it was to use the correct ropes and safety equipment.

"Nonsense," he laughed. "Real climbers prefer to manage without."

She thought his attitude was foolish but said nothing as she watched him run up another wall. They were little more than children really, she told herself with a sigh.

Her analysis of them was borne out when they left the castle for the nearby famous Cadwalader's ice cream shop. She ordered a plain cone for herself, Jake asked for a chocolate flake in his, but once again Danny and Steve had to outdo each other, requesting giant chocolate cones with three scoops each and every imaginable topping. The ice cream melted in the strong sun before they had even reached the beach, and long after Bel and Jake had finished their cones, Danny and Steve were licking chocolate sauce and toffee pieces off their hands. They were amply assisted by Lucy as they tried to stem the creamy cold, white melting tide with a soggy wafer bound in wet chocolate. In the end, Steve was the first to give up, and he threw what was left of his ice cream at a seagull who had been watching them hopefully from a safe distance. The bird screeched in delight, attracting a flurry of competition for the little piece of biscuit from five other similarly clamoring gulls.

"I think," Danny said seriously, "that if the theory of evolution and natural selection were true, then nature would already have favored a seagull that can eat quietly." He gave the last of his ice cream to the heartbroken dog who quickly dispatched it with a swift look at the treacherous master who had favored a mere bird. Danny was already bored with watching the spectacle of the fighting birds and angry dog, and he slipped off his shoes and socks as he hopped along the sand. Steve grinned as he saw him heading towards the waves and followed suit, and to Bel's chagrin so did Jake, handing his shoes to his mother without a word. She laughed to herself as she watched the three boys—for any difference in age between the Irishmen and Jake was purely temporal—race along in the shallows, dodging sun worshippers and throwing up showers of salt water, which quickly soaked them. Lucy bounded along between them in crazy zigzags, determined to trip at least one of them.

"They're all mad," Bel thought, but she was happy. The sand was warm between her toes and the sun shone as strongly as it might be expected to in August. The view of the Irish sea and the mountains was beautiful, and she felt safe here far away from Marty, who didn't even know where she was. It was a new life, a new beginning. She would take a few more days here drawing breath and recovering, and then she would begin in earnest the search for somewhere to live and work. When she was settled, she would contact a lawyer and begin the tedious process of working out what access Marty would need to Jake and what, if any, claim she would have on their meager savings. But she didn't want to think about all that now; she just wanted to enjoy being with Jake and their crazy new friends and even crazier dog.

It was strange to think she had only met them that morning. Both the young men were personable and pleasant, open and friendly, and she regarded them as old friends already. Steve had a depth and thoughtfulness about him that she liked despite his obvious immaturity in so many other respects. She could not imagine that it was his idea to be absent from work when he shouldn't; no doubt Danny had put him up to it. Steve was a loyal person, she thought, someone who could be trusted, someone a friend might turn to with a problem, knowing that he would empathize and go to all lengths to help. She sensed in Steve a profound sensitivity, and despite his posturing, a lack of self-confidence.

In contrast, Danny was supremely self-assured as well as quick-witted and alert, and in possession of considerable personal charm and magnetism. His bright brown eyes missed nothing and sparkled with laughter each time they met her own. His expression was one of confident nonchalance, but his frequent laugh was loud and hearty. He flirted boldly with her, tripping off wild compliments with a smile which dared her to believe he meant his words, but flattered her nevertheless.

Under different circumstances, she would like to have had them as friends, confided in them, told them about her oppressive marriage and eventual escape from her cruel husband. But she could not tell anyone just yet; it was still early, and she needed to settle her own feelings first.

CHAPTER 10

While Edward was being interviewed by President Chugg, Gwen was waiting in the main room of the rented hall. She had planned to use the time to go over the lessons she had learned and insights she had gained from that morning's meetings, an activity she had often found extremely helpful. On this occasion, however, Gwen was ashamed to acknowledge to herself that, except for Edward's original, insightful, and heartening talk, she had not really been listening or concentrating during sacrament meeting. She had been thinking and praying about Angela. After mulling over the situation for some time, Gwen determined that she would try to find time to speak to Angela, in hopes of bringing about a resolution of their difficulties. She would draw upon all her reserves of patience and forbearing in explaining to the younger woman how much she loved Edward, although the contemplation of Angela's possible responses frightened her a little. But the antipathy between them could not be allowed to fester.

Gwen tried to remind herself that any dialogue had to be an improvement, even if it only allowed both of them to express their opposing opinions. She had to do something, anyway. Those dear children were her grandchildren now, and while she had long ago accepted that she would never have children of her own, she was loathe to give up the possibility of grandchildren.

But it wasn't just Gwen's marriage to Edward that was a problem, she knew. It was Edward's adoption of her faith. Almost immediately after Edward had announced to his speechless children that he was dating again after five years as a widower, he had renounced the Anglican faith to which he had adhered all his life, and in which he had brought up his children, and joined a strange American sect they knew nothing about. It was hardly surprising they had been shocked, but that was almost a year ago now, and neither Ian nor Angela had spoken more than a few sentences to her since then.

Feeling her thoughts weighing her down, she decided to reread the letter that had arrived the day before and which she still had in her handbag.

Dear Gwen and Edward,

It was good to receive your letter and confirmation of your arrival next month. My family is looking forward to meeting you both and seeing these wonderful people who mean so much to me. The guest room here in Charlotte's home is already prepared for you, and I have made all the arrangements and confirmed with the temple the appointment for Edward's endowments and your sealing. I have taken a week off work so that I can be there with you and show you some of the sites, and also introduce you to my children and grandchildren. During the second week of your stay, you'll have to make your own entertainment as I have to be back at work. But there is plenty to do here in Salt Lake City, and I have a few guide books for you.

Charlotte and Larry are still enjoying their mission in Australia and seeing some wonderful growth there. Can you believe that they have met up again with the Michaelsons? Jonathan and Justin are touring Australia with Oscar, and they went to Perth to visit. Charlotte was really excited to see them, as you can imagine. Jonathan mentioned that they had received a wedding invitation from you but hadn't been able to attend.

I am sorry I could not be there for your wedding either, but I am thrilled that I will be for your sealing. You are both in my hearts. I think of you often and of Haven and the peace we found there.

With much love,
Megan Perant

The runners were at the end of the beach now, chasing and dodging waves as they waited for her to catch up. Jake had found a stick and was throwing it as far into the water as his young arms could manage so that Lucy could run headlong into the cold waves to fetch it. Each time she deposited the stick at his feet, she shook water all over him, but Jake just threw it again, laughing at the silly animal while his mother laughed at her silly, wet boy.

As Bel continued to pick her way through the contented sunbathers and happy children, doing her best not to destroy any of their sandcastles, she saw that the two young men had stopped chasing the dog and were talking conspiratorially, glancing at her occasionally with wide smiles. She blushed self-consciously as Danny laughed and declared, "Steve, food is definitely not the way to that particular woman's heart. Will you just look at how thin she is?"

Overcome with embarrassment, she looked away, trying to pretend she hadn't heard. As she did, she saw that she was not the only person watching the young lads with interest. Above them on the edge of the promenade, a tall, graying man sat on one of the public benches. He was peering round a wooden easel and squinting with barely concealed delight at Danny, Steve, Jake, and Lucy, noting each movement they made and brandishing his brush as he measured their relative heights and daubed excitedly at his canvas. Around his feet were bottles, tubes, and a selection of jam jars filled with water and brushes; his palette was plastic and fitted onto a holder on the side of the wooden easel. Interested passers-by stopped to look at his work, exclaiming in appreciation and then raising their eyes to the castle, which was evidently the primary subject of the piece.

Fascinated, as well as relieved at this diversion, Bel altered her course and headed up the slope to the promenade. She approached the artist quietly, not wanting to disturb his concentration, and murmured a quiet apology as she peered gingerly at what she could see of the painting.

Despite the faint pencil lines and great blank expanses of stretched paper, the painting promised to be exquisite. The parts that were already started demonstrated a powerful likeness of the mighty castle in pale watercolors, some fine detail of the houses at the base of the great mound, and a lively depiction of the beach in the foreground on which stick figures of two men, a boy, and a black Labrador played in the gleaming surf. Bel had never studied art but felt immediately that the figures playing on the beach among the oblivious sunbathers, overshadowed by the ancient fortress in the background, was a remarkable juxtaposition of the old and the new. The surrounding stone cottages, centuries old though some were modernized, served to join the past and present together. The artist had astonishing talent and, spellbound by the painting, Bel felt she needed to say something.

"That's lovely," she whispered, not wanting to disturb the man's concentration.

"Thank you," he replied, a clipped Scottish resonance reflected in his voice. As he spoke, she saw the muscles in his shoulders tense as his head pulled forward and down toward his chest, almost as if he were trying to hide. The movement reminded her of the stooping posture she had unconsciously adopted living with Marty, trying to escape his notice. She also saw the flush rising around the artist's ears, which told her that the man was shy and embarrassed at being addressed by a stranger. Feeling sympathy for him, she wondered whether she should carry on speaking to him or allow him his solitude, but she could imagine that others, less sensitive to his nervousness—those two elderly women, for example, who were watching with interest from a distance—would surely try to engage him in conversation when she moved away. She spoke gently and quietly, almost apologetically.

"Er . . . I'm with the group on the beach, the ones you're painting at the moment. Would you like them to stay a while longer or can we move on now?" She was pleased to see that he relaxed at her tone as she asked this.

"I'm most grateful to you," the man said quietly, and she leaned closer to hear him. "They actually answered a puzzle I'd been working on. I was trying to bring a bit more life into the foreground here and wasn't sure how to convey it. Most of the people on the beach are just lying around; they could be as dead as the people who once lived in the castle, and I really wanted to show some action and vitality. Then here came these two lively young men and a child and suddenly I knew the answer. Men spending time with children, not being afraid to show their more playful side."

Bel nodded in agreement that Danny, Steve, and Jake did indeed sum up the modern era. But he hadn't answered her question. Not wanting to prompt him, she simply watched and waited a while longer until he did.

"I don't really need them to be there anymore. It was enough for them to provide the inspiration and the framework. I can fill in the details anytime. You can be on your way if you like."

Bel was in no hurry. It was wonderful seeing how each stroke of the brush brought more life into the picture. "You're not from around here?" she ventured, wondering whether it was really appropriate to engage an artist in conversation, especially one evidently so reserved and ill at ease.

"No. I've come for a little holiday, get away from all the pressures of work and home, and just paint, you know."

"You don't paint for a living, then?"

He gave a wry laugh. "While you can earn money from painting, you can't make a living. No, I'm a solicitor—a lawyer—by profession. This is just my hobby." He waved his brush at the easel.

"Is your family with you, then?"

"No, it's pretty boring for my wife just leaving me to paint." He looked downcast for a moment and seemed to be considering whether he might say more. "I needed to be on my own, have some peace. It's kind of personal."

"I see. I'm sorry if I was intruding."

"Don't worry." He brushed away her apology. "I had already painted every scenic view in Scotland, I think, so I came to Wales. I think this particular view of Criccieth Castle has been painted a thousand times, but I still wanted to bring something new to it. I'll be back to finish it off tomorrow, weather permitting, and then there's a particularly nice valley scene further north I'll be having a go at."

"Well it's certainly a lovely painting. Best of luck with it. I'm so glad my friends and my son could help."

He looked at her as he nodded farewell, a tentative smile on his lips. He was a nice man, Bel thought, and a clever one. Not only was he clearly talented in art, but he was sensitive in his speech and showed a depth and attentiveness that no doubt explained the fine execution of detail in his painting.

As she made her way back down to the beach, Bel thought what a perfect day it had been and what a promising start to her new future. The young men were both great fun and good company, the weather was warm, and the visit to the castle and now the beach had been perfect. She had to thank Steve and Danny for inviting someone they barely knew on their excursion. Perhaps sometime she could repay the favor.

CHAPTER 11

When Edward and Gwen returned to Haven at two-thirty, Angela, Stuart, and the children were out and about, as indeed were all the guests. Edward offered at once to make them a light lunch, his face still shining with relief at having his talk now behind him, as much as with the excitement of what had transpired during his interview with President Chugg. As Edward disappeared into the kitchen, Gwen sat back in her favorite armchair, still thinking about Angela.

Some time later, Angela appeared, little Rosie in her arms, with Stuart behind her, holding Adam and Peter by the hands. The usually happy and lovable Rosie was crying, and Angela was trying desperately to comfort her, but without success. Standing up, Gwen offered Angela the comfortable armchair and asked, "Shall I hold her for you for a moment so you can rest?"

"No thank you," Angela said curtly, and Gwen thought she saw an apology in Stuart's eyes for his wife's ill-mannered behavior earlier.

"Does she need feeding? Can I warm a bottle for you? They're in the fridge."

The younger woman's mouth began to form another "No," but since it was Gwen's kitchen, after all, and a tiresome task to boot, she simply nodded and sank down in the chair.

In the kitchen Edward was busy microwaving two ready-meals. He glanced at Gwen quizzically as she entered, and Gwen confirmed that Angela and Stuart had arrived back from their mountain walk. Warming the bottle carefully in a jug of hot water as per Angela's strict instructions to Edward that very morning, Gwen tested the temperature of the formula on her wrist, then carried it out to where the tired mother was waiting.

"Would you like me to feed her for you? You could have a bit of a lie down." Gwen badly wanted Angela to agree but suspected that she would never let Gwen hold her child, an assumption that proved entirely correct as Angela snatched the bottle and tipped it into the baby's eager mouth without a word. Stuart and the two boys had disappeared upstairs, but Angela seemed comfortable in the armchair. Gwen took a seat on the sofa opposite, still wearing her best smile, a mask to hide her nervousness.

"The weather's been so beautiful today, and the sky is so clear. You must have enjoyed a lovely view on your walk."

Apparently Angela wasn't interested in small talk. It was time, Gwen decided, to say what needed to be said, something that would address the problems between them and bring them out into the open. She offered a quick, nervous prayer for the right words and a loving spirit before speaking. "I think you're usually such a warm and thoughtful person, Angela. Why do you dislike me so much?"

It had the desired effect. Gwen immediately had Angela's full attention. Her stepdaughter stared at her with something close to incredulity, but she took her time before replying. It was better that way, Gwen thought. She wanted Angela to consider her words carefully since what she said next was so important to their future relationship.

"Because you took my father away from us, away from all he believed in and all that was important to him. You got him to adopt your weird religion, probably by blackmailing him into it and saying you wouldn't marry him if he didn't. And now you seem to think that gives you the right to be my mother and my children's grandmother."

It was the reply Gwen had expected, a reason she might have worked out for herself, and yet she was unsatisfied with this answer. Angela's barely disguised contempt of Gwen had led her to suspect there was something more, something deeper and more difficult to guess and certainly much more difficult for Angela to voice. But prying too much further at such an early and sensitive stage, Gwen decided, might be unwise.

"Your father is such a good and loving man, Angela, and I can understand why you are unhappy not to have him living near you now. We shared him for many years, didn't we, you and I? I saw him for only a few weeks each year, and you lived close to him the rest of the time. I know how you feel because I'm sure he's told you that I've loved him for some years, and I did used to miss him so much during those times."

"Great, so you won in the end." Angela's tone was truculent. "Bully for you. It doesn't mean I'm obliged to like you."

"Of course not, but Edward loves me and it hurts him that you don't. Perhaps if we spent a little more time together, we could learn to understand one another."

The younger woman looked at Gwen in amazement. "I don't have to spend time with you," she objected. "I don't have to try to like you. I don't even have to see you. You're not my mother. I don't owe you anything."

"But you owe your father respect, and if you love him, you should want him to be happy."

At that, Angela flushed red with anger. "Oh, so I'm not capable of making him happy, am I? He was miserable all those years he lived in Birmingham, was he? You're just an old, lonely, twisted religious freak who saw a vulnerable, rich widower and thought she could just waltz in and be part of his big happy family."

"Angela! How dare you speak to Gwen like that?" Edward had come into the room and was more angry than Gwen had ever seen him. He placed a protective and comforting hand on Gwen's shoulder as he scolded his daughter. "I didn't bring you up to be that unkind to anyone, let alone my wife. Now if Rosie's finished her bottle, I suggest you take her upstairs and don't come down until you've a civil tongue in your head."

Like a penitent child, Angela obeyed with a scowl but not a word. As she climbed the stairs, Edward silently kissed the top of his wife's head in apology for his display of anger as much as for his daughter's behavior. He was such a good father, Gwen thought. She hated for any contention to come into her home, and she was shaking a little, unused to such scenes and alarmed at the depth of Angela's feelings.

And yet, it had not been a total disaster. Gwen had put her case well and had not descended to anger, but there was obviously something more to the situation than Angela was admitting.

Edward moved round to sit beside Gwen, his concerned eyes searching her face. "Our food is ready; in fact, it might have gone cold. I was just on the other side of the door, and I didn't want to interrupt when you seemed to be doing so well with her for a few minutes there. I'll just pop it back into the microwave." He kissed her again as he spoke, and she smiled weakly up at him.

Years ago Angela had asked him why he kept returning to Haven after her mother's death. At some point she had begun speculating on his feelings for Haven's proprietress, and for that reason, Edward thought his daughter could hardly have been surprised when he announced his courtship and plans to remarry. But Angela's intense and jealous dislike of Gwen seemed to be more than was warranted, even by the reasons she had given. It was a puzzle to him.

Brian McNaught took his dinner in his room again that night. He had been out all day, arriving back just before six and immediately going upstairs unseen. Gwen would not have known he was even there were it not for his car outside, still packed full of mysterious boxes and lengths of wood. As she placed his tray on the tallboy, Gwen considered extending to him the invitation to family home evening that she would shortly offer in the dining room. However, she dismissed the thought immediately, certain of his reaction and not wanting a repeat of the scene that morning.

He thanked her politely for the meal, and she nodded in acknowledgment but made no attempt at pleasantries. It was too bad, she thought sadly. She would have liked to talk to him, ask about his home life, whether he'd had a good day and where he'd been, what all the stuff was in his car that he had not bothered to unload. Perhaps she would try again tomorrow.

The scene in the dining room was an altogether happier one if only because Belinda Hunt was doing her best to carry on a conversation with Danny O'Hanlon and Steve Collins on the farthest table, which required raised voices and led to misunderstandings when accents or the natural quietness of Bel's speech confused what was said. The lads seemed to find this as hilarious as they found everything else, and their lively joviality more than made up for the strained silence maintained by Angela and Stuart.

Dinner was served and enjoyed, and as she was clearing the plates, Gwen made her customary announcement. "Everyone, we have a tradition at Haven and in the Church that Monday night is family home evening night. This means we all gather in the lounge for some activities and learning and refreshments so we can get to know each other better. It's usually good fun, and I'd like to invite you all to join us." Again she looked meaningfully at Angela. "I thought tomorrow it might be fun to do a talent night and give everyone a few minutes to display their skills and talents. It might be singing or playing an instrument or perhaps just talking about something you excel at or prizes you have won. Then we'll conclude with a little thought, and we'll enjoy some refreshments together."

"Sounds like a laugh," Danny said, nudging his friend and grinning.

"Count us in!" Steve called impulsively, and Jake echoed him from beside his mother, who pulled a face of exasperation even though she had been thinking of attending anyway.

Edward looked severely at Angela, who could not bring herself to display any enthusiasm or actually speak, but at least nodded, unsmiling, at Gwen. Her agreement might be under duress, but Gwen was nevertheless pleased that the family would be in attendance. It would almost mean a full house—if it weren't for the mysterious and enigmatic Brian McNaught.

CHAPTER 12

Bel slipped out of dinner early to telephone her sister Amy, having already spoken of it with Mrs. Anderton and offered her some money—which was refused—to cover the cost of the call. Her fingers trembled and her heart pounded in her chest as she dialed the number, and she had to keep reminding herself that this was only her sister, not Marty. And yet it was too close to home. Haven was a world away, and Bel somehow felt as if she was giving up the safety of her new life even thinking of her old one. But she had always been close to her sister and knew she would be worried.

"Amy?"

"Hello . . . Lindy?" Concern, love, and relief were all condensed into one word.

"Yes, it's me. Jake is with me, too."

"Are you all right? Where are you? I mean, is everything . . ."

"We're fine, but I can't tell you where just yet. We're a good many miles away, in a guest house at the moment, but we'll be finding somewhere more permanent in a few days. When we're settled I'll let you know our address. I just need a bit of time to get over this first bit."

"Of course, I understand. Oh, Lindy, well done! I'm so pleased you've done it at last. I miss you, but I couldn't stand to see you so miserable."

Bel had known Amy would understand, but still the obvious delight in her voice was wonderful to hear. It was all the sanction and affirmation she needed.

"Has Marty said anything to you?"

"He called round yesterday with that Neanderthal brother of his, said he'd been to Mum's and to a few friends, but no one knew where you were. I didn't either, of course. He seemed angry and irritated, but no more than you'd expect. I told him I didn't know anything, which was true at the time. I'm pretty sure he believed me; he could see how worried I was. Do you want me to let people know you're okay?"

"Yes, please, particularly Mum, of course. You could let Marty know if you like. Just tell him my solicitor will be in touch. I'll be divorcing him, so I don't need to see him ever again." It was so wonderful to be able to say that!

"How did you do it, Lindy? Why didn't you tell me what you were planning? Have you got enough money? Did you go on the train? Why did you just disappear like that?"

"I've been saving up for a long time. I bought a little car, just an old wreck with enough life in it to get us here. I picked it up on Friday and parked it in the next street. I had to go overnight. I couldn't face packing and leaving in plain view, telling him we were going. I didn't think he'd let us leave quietly."

"Well done, Lindy. I am proud of you."

"I have to go now, Amy. People are coming into the room. I'll call again soon, I promise." She placed the receiver down again, smiling to herself and feeling better than she had for years. She had done it. They were free.

Marty was getting bored with fish and chips. This was the third time he'd eaten them, straight from the container, since Lindy had gone. He still couldn't fathom the finer points of cooking and could see himself surviving on take-aways and cold baked beans for the rest of his life. There hadn't been any decent matches on television over the weekend. All he had to do was watch the clock as he threw more vinegar on his chips and waited for eight o'clock to come round so he could go out with Paul.

It wasn't that he missed her exactly. It was just that it was dull without her and the boy around. His initial anger had passed into confusion, as he wondered why she could possibly want to run off like that. He provided for her, spent hours every day installing kitchens and repairing washing machines so that she could buy nice things for herself. He took care of her, and he'd given her the child he knew all women wanted, and a roof over her head. The romance had gone out of their marriage, he freely admitted, and he knew that at times he had behaved rather badly towards her, although mostly he had been drunk and so couldn't be held responsible for his actions. Still, he was her husband.

His chips had gone cold. He squelched them into a mushy ball inside their paper and aimed it badly at the bin, so it bounced off the edge and onto the floor. He would be glad when she was back, and he could eat proper meals again. She had to come back, he knew. She had no money. She'd never worked a day in her life and she had no marketable skills, so how could she possibly get a job to support herself? A week, maybe two, and she'd have to come home. But he thought it would also help to find her and offer some gentle persuasion. He found it frustrating not knowing where she was or how long this silly business was going to go on.

The telephone broke into his miserable silence and startled him. He answered it.

"Hello, Martin."

It was a woman's voice, one he ought to recognize, but didn't. It wasn't his wife anyway.

"It's Amy. I've heard from Lindy."

He grunted acknowledgment. He didn't like Amy. He didn't like any of her family really. "When's she bringing my boy home?" he asked.

"She's not. She just wanted me to let you know that they're both safe and well. Her solicitor will be in touch shortly about the divorce. That's all. Good-bye." A click, a hum, and she was gone.

Marty sat deep in thought for a few minutes, noticing how the dust had begun to gather and the cobwebs were once again stretching across the high corners. He picked up the phone again and dialed the number he knew best.

"Paul. Marty."

"Marty, hi. Still on for tonight?"

"Paul, Amy's rung. She's heard from Lindy. But she won't say where they are. Reckons Lindy's divorcing me."

Paul commiserated in his usual aggressive fashion by calling Amy a few abusive names. Then he stopped suddenly, as though he had an idea. "Is she the one who did Lindy that birthday party last year?"

Marty remembered it well. Paul had drunk too much and nearly got into a fight with Amy's boyfriend. Lindy had driven Marty and Paul home before the party had ended, both of them laughing all the way because they knew they would never see the boring boyfriend again anyway, the way Amy went through them. "Yeah, why?"

"She's got one of those telephone display things. I remember seeing it."

"What telephone display things?" Marty had no clue what he was talking about or how it might help bring his woman back. Paul had always been the intellectual one.

"It shows you the number of the person who's ringing, and it stores them and shows you the last few calls. We can go to Amy's, and if you can distract her a few minutes, I can have a look at it. If we can get the number, we can find out where they are."

It was a brilliant plan. With a telephone number, they could get some idea of where she was. Marty wasn't sure how, exactly, and wondered what they would do if it turned out to be a call box on a motorway service station, but he had enough confidence in his older brother to assume he knew what he was going to do with the number when he had it. Marty asked no more questions, except to enquire when they might carry out their plan.

"No rush, we don't want to make her suspicious. Perhaps tomorrow. Lindy's bound to call her again soon. She used to ring her nearly every day, didn't she, wasting your money on the phone bill?"

Marty felt quite excited about it all as he laughed with his brother over their cunning scheme. They were like detectives. True to their family name, they were going to hunt his wife down, they were going to find her, and they were going to bring her back.

Bel awakened to a fine sunny morning, sparkling rays casting warm light across the beamed ceiling of her cozy bedroom. According to the clock on the dresser, there was no need to hurry out of bed. All the same, she could not shake the feeling that something was terribly wrong. She should have been content, relaxed, and happy, for she had drifted into a restful sleep in a cheerful mood last night.

She sat bolt upright and knew instantly what it was. Jake was gone. Stunned for a moment, she stared at his empty bed. It was crumpled and unmade, his pajamas cast roughly across it and his shoes gone from below it. Bel was dressed in a minute and running her fingers through her hair—there was no time to bother with a brush—as she hurried out onto the landing, calling Jake's name without even thinking she might wake the other guests. She continued down the stairs, calling him more urgently, then through into the dining room, her heart thumping. Perhaps she would find him there, waiting patiently for his breakfast. But she saw only Mr. and Mrs. Anderton putting butter and milk out on the tables. They looked up in surprise when Bel entered, saw the panic in her eyes, and heard Jake's name die on her lips. Gwen rushed over and put an arm around Bel's heaving shoulders.

"Jake's gone," she said, her breath coming in fearful gasps. "When I woke up, he was gone."

"Now don't worry. Calm down a little," Gwen spoke soothingly. "He's probably just in the garden enjoying the sunshine." She steered Bel to the deep armchair in the lounge and sat her down as she asked her husband to fetch a glass of warm milk. "Edward, perhaps you should stay with her while I check the garden and the paths. Now don't worry, dear, I'll have a good search and bring him back in to you in just a moment."

Bel sat absorbed in a growing fear and panic, afraid to admit to what she was almost certain had happened. It was Marty and Paul. Marty didn't really care about her; she had known that for years, but he wanted his son back. Somehow they had come to get him in the night. They had learned where she was staying, and they had come to Haven and taken Jake. She could not imagine how, but in her despair at knowing Marty would never let her see him again, she did not stop to wonder how he had found them or how he could have come into their room and taken his son without a sound.

In her heart she silently called Jake's name over and over again in desperation, longing for him. But it appeared he was nowhere in the house. He was only just five years old and so adventurous. There was a road just down that driveway. What if Marty and Paul had come for her and parked outside, waiting and planning, and then Jake had wandered outside . . . ?

Edward Anderton arrived back with the warm milk, and Bel drank it without even tasting it. Angela and Stuart Kirby, awakened by Bel's frantic calling, came down the stairs looking puzzled, Angela carrying baby Rosie and Stuart leading the toddler by the hand as little Peter followed behind. Seeing the whole and happy family, and in particular the little boy so close to Jake's age, was more than Bel could bear, and she began to sob desperately.

She was able to compose herself after a few moments, reassured by the older man's comforting arm around her. She was also beginning to think how unlikely it was that anyone could have taken Jake without him protesting and thus disturbing her sleep. Still, she needed to be able to discount that possibility. Through her tears, she turned to her host.

"Has anyone been here? Two men, one bald, the other with brown hair and a moustache? Both big men. They might have asked for me?"

Edward shook his head in bewilderment, and for a moment that was some comfort until his wife came back, alone, her face troubled. Bel began to weep again.

Seeing the scene before her, Angela turned to her father. "What's going on?"

"The little boy has gone missing," Edward replied gently.

Her heart went out to the young blonde woman. "Is there anything I can do to help?"

"I've checked all around the gardens and down the drive," Gwen said. "But if we all look, we could cover a good part of the lower mountain slopes. He might have wandered off somewhere, but he can't have gone far. We have to start looking quickly. If we can't find him in the next half hour, I'll call my brother Llifon. He's with the mountain rescue."

CHAPTER 13

I t had already been half an hour since Bel had awakened to find Jake gone, and Bel listened with growing terror to this new proposal. She could not get out of her mind the certainty that Marty had found them and had taken Jake, despite Edward's assurances and her recognition of how improbable it was. She listened as the Andertons and the Kirbys made hasty plans. Gwen was to stay behind with Bel and the children, and telephone mountain rescue at exactly eight-thirty. Edward would search the north slope and the mountain path. Angela and Stuart would check along the driveway and the road at the bottom. The weather was good, so Jake was in no danger of freezing, Edward noted. He was just lost. That was some comfort at least, even to his mother who, despite herself, remained convinced that he had been kidnapped.

A loud barking made everyone look up, and at that same moment Danny and Steve burst through the front door. A muddy Lucy bounded in excitedly behind them, and just behind her was Jake, laughing and chasing the dog.

"Just in time for breakfast!" Danny cried, then stopped as he saw the group of pale, worried people in the center of the room. His eyes took in the hunched figure of Bel, her eyes red and her face streaked with frightened tears. Beside her was Angela, who had been trying to comfort her. Bel saw Jake at that moment and flew across the room to hug him to her, crying anew at the joy of seeing him. Jake let his mother put her arms around him, but he seemed rather uncomfortable with it all, since five was really too old to have his mother display such affection before strangers whose attention was riveted on him.

"What's going on?" Steve ventured tentatively.

"We were worried about the boy. His mother didn't know where he was," Gwen answered levelly.

Steve flushed a bright red as he realized the significance of those words. He said nothing more, just shook his head and ran his fingers through his hair as he looked, embarrassed, at the still sobbing Bel.

"He saw us leaving with Lucy this morning, taking her for her early morning walk. He asked if he could come too, and we assumed he'd asked his mother . . ." Danny's voice trailed off.

"You were asleep," Jake protested to Bel, pulling away from her embrace.

"You should have wakened me. You know you must always let me know where you're going. I thought— I thought . . ." She could say nothing more, overcome with relief at having him back. Marty had not taken him away. Jake had merely gone for a walk with their new friends, that was all. She looked first at Steve and then Danny, her anger and disappointment in them evident, and they felt the full force of her steely gaze and were taken aback by it.

"Well, we're all very happy to have you safe, Jake," Mrs. Anderton said. "I'm sure you're hungry. Breakfast is served." She hurried back into the kitchen.

Bel's legs still felt unsteady as she walked, half dazed, into the dining room, clutching Jake's hand. She said nothing for some time, breathing deeply, trying to restore her equilibrium. Danny and Steve were unusually quiet at their table, too. Danny hardly touched his breakfast and Steve could not raise his eyes from his plate. She managed to feel a little sorry for them; after all, they were little more than boys themselves with no idea of the responsibility and wrenching love that goes with raising a child. It probably hadn't crossed their minds that Jake hadn't asked permission when they called to him to join them on their walk in the early morning sunshine. And they didn't know, of course, that Bel was fearful of a man who wanted Jake back or that she was sure with every passing minute that he drew ever nearer.

After breakfast they took up their usual places in the lounge. By now Bel had calmed down enough to agree that Jake could leave her sight to go up to Danny and Steve's room to play with Steve's computer game, although she watched him as he climbed the stairs with Steve until she could no longer see them and then listened carefully for the squeaking of the door to the room. Danny watched her doing this and gently suggested that Bel sit and rest for a while longer. Bel was still feeling a little unsteady and was happy to rest on the comfortable sofa before she went upstairs to prepare for the day's job hunting. As she flipped through the TV listings magazine, Danny came and sat beside her without a hint of nervousness or hesitation.

"Bel, I'm really sorry. I didn't think. I hope you can forgive me."

All credit to him, she thought. No excuses, no attempt to share the blame with Steve. He admitted he was wrong and apologized without even expecting that this automatically excused him. She had calmed down now, pushed thoughts of Marty away so that she could think rationally. It had only been half an hour, after all, and Jake had only been walking the dog with Danny and Steve. Jake had been most to blame; he knew that he should have told her where he was going. Danny had been foolish, but he had meant well. He had really thought he was giving her a break and making the child happy, and he was charming when he was contrite. Her heart went out to him.

"I overreacted," she said quietly. "I should have been more reasonable. He's five now and quite sensible. I'm sorry too, it's just . . . I have a lot on my mind."

"Oh?" Danny asked, waiting for an explanation of this, but Bel said nothing more despite his prompting. He seemed to realize he would get nothing more and went on, "Thank you for forgiving me. I act before I think, sometimes. I have a lot to learn."

She agreed heartily with that and nodded, then laughed at his attempt to feign a hurt expression. Hearing her laughter, he was glad. The sight of her despair and the realization that he was to blame had shocked him to the core. He found her a sweet, affable girl, easy to talk to, trusting, and intelligent. He liked her and had wondered yesterday at some of the strange dichotomies about her. He hoped to have some of his questions answered before too long. Now, however, he had more questions, not less.

"Anything on TV tonight?" he asked, looking over her shoulder at the *Radio Times*. At the same moment they exclaimed, "*Frontier!*" and then laughed at each other.

"You like it, too?" she asked, astonished.

"Love it. It's my favorite program. It's not on the Irish channels, but we can get it with satellite. It's getting quite exciting at the moment, too, with Captain Bennett still held captive in the seascape and the fifth-moon war about to break out."

She had never met anyone else who liked *Frontier* before. It was a strange brand of science-fiction soap opera, rooted to one planet and therefore of little interest to true science fiction fans, but firmly set in outer space in the future, so rather too offbeat for soap-opera watchers. She was pleased to find someone who liked it as much as she did. Marty had hated it. He always went out when she was watching it.

"I love the way it shows how people in the future still have the same complexities and inadequacies that we do, but then they have more to contend with as they struggle to colonize a hostile world," she said, her enthusiasm spilling over.

"I hope this family home evening thing is finished in time for us to watch it," Danny said. "Any ideas what you might do for it?"

She shrugged. She hadn't really thought about it. "I dance a little. I've been going to ballet classes since I was young, but there's not really enough space here . . ."

She saw a smile cross his face and he nodded as though his suspicions were confirmed. "I thought you were a dancer. You're so delicate yet elegant, and you move so gracefully. Are you sure you couldn't dance for us here? I'd love to see you perform."

She laughed, waving aside his praise, and reflected that he certainly knew what to say to flatter and delight a woman. His dark hooded eyes did not leave hers for a moment as he spoke, and yet, for the first time since she had met him yesterday morning, she doubted his motives and honesty. Perhaps she was simply unused to receiving compliments, she thought. She would not yet allow herself to wonder whether Danny O'Hanlon might actually be attracted to her. She assured him that she was quite certain there was not enough room, and that anyway, she hadn't brought her shoes. She would think about what other talent she might demonstrate.

He flashed that winning smile. "I'm sure you have lots of talents."

Bel shook her head. "I used to do recitations at school. I suppose I could read a poem or something. It's not very exciting, but at least it's easy and won't take much time to practice. I'll ask Mrs. Anderton if she's got any good poetry books I could borrow."

"Sounds great," he said. "But I'd rather see you dance."

She was unsure of how to respond and simply shrugged. Sensing the awkwardness, Danny moved on. "Steve already knows what he's going to do tonight."

"Oh? What's that?"

"Mrs. Anderton mentioned refreshments and that happens to be his talent. He's going to put on his chef's hat and prepare something really spectacular for us to nibble on as we listen to everyone singing. I suggested it to him last night, and he seemed quite taken with the idea, probably because it's preferable to having to perform in some way or the other. Mrs. Anderton was really pleased, too. She's more than happy to let him have the kitchen."

Despite the huge breakfast she had just eaten, Bel found her mouth watering at the thought of some delicious, professionally made hors d'oeuvres. The mountain air seemed to have made her far hungrier that she ever was at home.

"What about you?" she asked Danny. "Do you have any talents?"

"I can drink a pint of Guinness straight down in fifteen seconds. That's less time than it takes to pour it!"

"I don't think that would be appropriate," she said, trying not to smile at his boyish boastfulness.

"I can switch on the television in my room at home by throwing a dart at it."

This time she looked impressed. "Did you bring anything with you?"

"No. Not even the darts."

"Too bad," she said. "Anything else?"

"I can juggle, as long as it's with one ball at a time."

"Can you sing?" she suggested.

"Oh, sure," he grinned. "Unless you're one of these cultured types who like it to be in tune."

She was exasperated now. "Seriously, you must be good at something."

"I can ride a horse, paddle a canoe, climb, play pool, drive a tractor, milk a cow. I know a bit about wine, and I speak two languages. In fact, I'm thinking I might go with milking the cow, but I don't trust Steve not to chop it up and barbecue it afterwards."

She laughed at this, thinking how witty and funny he was and how much she enjoyed listening to him. Still, she was painfully aware of how dull and quiet she must seem to him in comparison. It gave her an idea, however, a delightful thought which seemed right and perfect for him.

"Why don't you do a comedy act? Just a few minutes standup."

He roared with laughter at her suggestion. "Yeah, great, my speciality is catching rotten fruit."

"Well, I think you've kissed the Blarney stone," she said, amazed to find herself actually teasing him.

"For me to do ten minutes of standup comedy off the top of my head tonight, I'd need to do more than just kiss the blasted rock. I'd need to have *married* it."

She looked askance at him, eyebrows raised, and understanding her expression, he grinned in excitement. He could do it, with her help, and he began to feel rather excited at the prospect. He was a natural extrovert and he loved a challenge. He had applied his razor-sharp wit to humor ever since it had languished, under-stimulated, in the classrooms of his youth. Seeing his eyes narrow as his mind went into overdrive, planning his act, Bel hugged herself with delight. She was looking forward to that evening already, knowing that listening to Danny would be a treat. He would be a natural. Perhaps she had known him only one day, but she had no doubt that he was a brilliant and rare man. She tried not to compare him with Marty, but it was obvious he had ten times the worth of her husband. Even though she had fallen in love with Marty once, Danny was something else again. He had already made her forget the fear she had felt when her son seemed to be lost—and that he had been responsible for it.

CHAPTER 14

Gwen was feeling quite hopeful and optimistic again by midmorning. She had been shocked and upset to learn that Bel's son was missing, and alarmed at the terror she saw in the mother's face. Her automatic response had been to pray for the child's safe return and also to ask for strength for his mother and wisdom for herself in handling the frightening situation. All those prayers had been answered, for Bel had been restored to her peaceful and gentle self very quickly and seemed none the worse for her scare. Even now she was chatting happily with Danny O'Hanlon, who had surely learned a little wisdom himself. Jake was safe and well, and Gwen had been able to set aside her own fears, comforting Bel and organizing the thankfully unnecessary search when she might so easily have panicked or done nothing.

Added to the pleasure she felt at the happy outcome of the crisis was the ease with which she and Angela had joined forces to allocate duties of searching, and the readiness with which Angela had acknowledged Gwen as the best person to stay at Haven with the children in case Jake returned, and to coordinate their efforts. During the emergency they had spoken to each other without anger, which had given Gwen some confidence that they could do so again to put their differences behind them.

Then, when Steven Collins had asked if he might be in charge of making the refreshments for that evening, Gwen had been delighted to show him the kitchen. She invited him to have a free hand, and she looked forward to the undoubtedly delicious results as much as to having a break from making bara brith and welshcakes. Her hopeful mood continued all morning, even in spite of Brian McNaught's complaint that his breakfast was late. He had evidently failed to notice the unfolding drama downstairs, and she did not bother to enlighten him.

The washing up was finished at last, the dining room re-laid, and the floors vacuumed. She would wait until all the guests were gone out for the day before she went up to straighten and clean their rooms. Brian McNaught had left even before she returned to collect his tray and she wondered where he went all day by himself. She sat quietly by the fireplace with her notepad and pen, carefully listing the things she and Edward would need to take with them on their trip to America. There seemed to be so much to remember, from their marriage certificate and passports, to spare film for the camera and their address book for postcards. As she studied her list, Edward joined her, offering a few additional suggestions, and then laughed as Gwen wrote plainly for him to see, "Note: Buy bigger suitcase."

"I was pleased that Angela agreed to come to family home evening tonight," Gwen said suddenly.

Edward did not miss the question behind the statement. He coughed and looked severe for a moment. "I asked her to. After the way she spoke to you yesterday, I think she owes you a little respect. She is still my daughter and still has to do as she's told sometimes."

Gwen was a little perturbed by his answer. "So it's her punish-ment then, is it? Do you think that's the right attitude to family home evening?"

He shook his head. "That's not how I see it. You've been holding these open-invitation home evenings ever since I can remember, usually on your own, but sometimes, when others chose to come along, they have been excellent, like last year when we all helped Charlotte and Megan with their family history. None of those people were members of your family, not even me. But Angela and Stuart and the children are, and they of all people should be there."

Gwen nodded, pleased that they would almost have full house attendance, were it not for the last guest, the strangely rude and mysterious Scot.

"I haven't said anything to Brian McNaught. I wonder whether I should." When Edward did not offer any comment, she added, "We really don't know anything about him. His car is packed with something that he's never bothered to unload. He eats in his room and never speaks to anyone. And he is out all day. I wonder if there's something wrong? Perhaps when he comes back tonight, I should try speaking to him, ask him if I can be of any help."

She looked at her husband, but he was quiet, his eyes focused on the list she still held. She could tell, however, that he was not reading it. "Do you think I should talk to him, dear?"

He drew a deep breath and looked at her. "No, I don't think you should."

"But he might be lonely—"

"Gwen, my love, you are such a kind and honest person," Edward smiled at her gently. "You have done a great deal for many of the visitors who have come here by sharing your wisdom and your love with them, and I know they will always remember you with gratitude. But Mr. McNaught has asked for peace and quiet, and I think that's what we ought to give him."

Gwen looked thoughtful. "I don't really mind that he might be a little impolite—" She stopped at the look Edward gave her.

"I get the feeling there's more to his strange behavior and attitude than we might realize," he said soberly. "I know that you reach out to these people because they are your brothers and sisters. You really care for them, and I have seen just how many times you have touched their lives and brought them happiness and understanding. But I have the feeling that to someone like Brian McNaught, your interest in him may be interpreted as nosiness. He might feel you're preaching to him."

Gwen stared at Edward, speechless and hurt. She couldn't believe he would actually criticize her dealings with her guests, that he would say she was nosy and preached at people, and that she was wrong to want to help Brian McNaught. She knew now why Angela had agreed to attend home evening when faced with her father's rebuke.

Gwen shut her eyes tightly, not wanting to look at her husband. He had never spoken to her like this, had never suggested that anything she did at Haven was not exactly as it should be done. She wanted to ignore his words and follow her own inclinations to speak to Mr. McNaught when he returned. But, she reminded herself, her husband had also had a great deal of experience dealing with people, and as a man, perhaps he understood something about Brian McNaught that she herself could not see.

Still, she was overcome with humiliation that her husband would find fault with her and feel the need to correct her actions. It was especially hard to accept when she had been on her own for so long. She swallowed, remembering that in just over a month they would be sealed for eternity in the temple. Would eternity be like this, her husband finding fault with her every move?

"Just . . . leave it for now," Edward begged, laying a gentle hand on hers and feeling her flinch away from him. He could see how unsettled she was, but he had needed to say what he had. Now, not knowing what else to do, he excused himself, found his gardening gloves, and went outside to do some therapeutic weeding.

***

In her panic at losing her son, Bel had dressed in a hurry this morning, not bothering to wash or brush her hair. Now it felt good to freshen up and tie back her long hair at a leisurely pace, knowing that Jake was safe and oblivious to everything except Steve's computer game. Looking in the full-length mirror, she saw that the color had returned to her cheeks and her eyes had regained their old sparkle. The Welsh air had done her good, and her new freedom from Marty's tyranny had already gone a good way to restoring her strength and good humor. She managed to smile at the reflected image, pleased to see her skin looking so clear and radiant and her hair shining, although she was still rather too thin.

She called in at Steve and Danny's room to collect Jake and was invited to join them while the boy finished his game, ably assisted by Danny, who whooped a juvenile victory cry every time one of the androids was dispatched. Bel felt rather giddy as she sat on Danny's bed, where Steve sat beside her, talking to her as best he could over the bleeps, whistles, and electronic music of the noisy computer game plugged into the portable television.

She found herself blushing as Steve spoke and she laughed inwardly at herself as she noted his strong chin and low, harmonious voice. He was one of the finest-looking men she had ever seen, strongly built and with elegant features, but she knew that what most recommended him to her was his admiration of her son's ability. He described how quickly Jake had picked up the game, how fearlessly he had played with Lucy, and what a sweet-natured child he was.

This is ridiculous, Bel scolded herself. She liked Steve very much, of course. He was sensitive and kind, though moody at times; she already knew much of his personality and liked all that she had discovered. But he was young and they were just friends, nothing more. As he discussed his plans for a delicate and exotic selection of canapés for that evening, she admired him all the more, seeing how well he knew his craft.

She wondered at herself as she caught herself hanging on his every word. Starved for affection for many years and vulnerable, she shouldn't be surprised at her enjoyment of the company of these two friendly young men. It had been many years since a man had spoken so freely and kindly to her, and both Steve and Danny had a great deal of charm. But she thought she might like them in any circumstance. They made it clear that they valued her opinions and enjoyed her company. They liked her for herself, not from any obligation to her or for what she could offer to them. She found it a new and wonderful experience. There were good men in the world, too.

She looked up to find Steve watching her and she blushed. "Sorry, I was thinking and I just sort of got lost in my thoughts."

He nodded sympathetically. "You know, I've been wondering why it is you say so little about yourself. What's the big secret?"

She looked away. "Nothing I want to talk about."

"Perhaps I can help?"

"No, thank you."

"Hey." He smiled, showing two rows of perfect white teeth in that handsome face. "You can tell me." He laid a comforting hand on her shoulder. It felt good there. His attention felt good. But she mustn't; she had resolved to say nothing. She repeated her refusal with some difficulty as she fought against the longing to unburden to this delightful man.

He seemed disappointed, and for a moment she thought he wanted to want to press further, but eventually he shrugged and turned his attention back to the game. She hoped she had not offended him by refusing to discuss her past. Both Steve and Danny had become close friends in the last day or so, and it was only natural that they were concerned for her. But she had felt so free here at Haven, and she was reluctant to spoil this new world of hers by opening the door to the past and letting it intrude upon her present.

"Listen," he said, changing the subject, "we've got to hit the shops today, buy some of the things I'll need for tonight. You want to come?"

She was pleased to note that he didn't sound hurt or concerned at her reticence, and the thought of a day's shopping was infinitely more appealing than traipsing round the job centers. That task could wait for another day. She accepted with gratitude and, excusing herself, she slipped back to her room and emptied the few sticky tubes and dusty cases from her makeup bag in a clatter all over the tallboy. Squinting at herself in the mirror, she began applying them with considerable care, then freed her hair from its plait and pulled a brush through it until it floated with the static. She wished she had thought to have it trimmed before leaving Sussex.

"Mum?" Jake had come looking for her. Unused to seeing his mother wearing makeup, he stared in surprise.

Seeing the bewilderment on his face, Bel stared back at him. Suddenly she realized how foolish she was being. She never wore makeup; she had only brought it along so that she could look her best for job interviews. Whatever had possessed her to think she needed it now? She hugged her son, laughing, then went to the sink in the corner of the room and scrubbed it all off again. She was ready for another day out with her two new friends, but she would be her own true self.

CHAPTER 15

G wen would have liked some peace that morning. For once she did not welcome the company of her guests as her mind was still turning over what Edward had said. She felt something close to anguish as she thought she remembered the harsh tone to his voice, but then Steven had interrupted her thoughts to ask her where they might find a good delicatessen and where they could buy fresh seafood or gather samphire, and he was followed by Bel Hunt, who had sought her out trying to find something to read for that evening.

Gwen took a deep breath and tried to put aside the hurt she felt over what might be considered her first disagreement with Edward. Bel Hunt was a sweet young woman, a little shy and at times strangely out of step and disconnected from the world around her, but she was clearly bright and honest and touchingly devoted to her son. She deserved the best Gwen could give her, however difficult Gwen might find it to assume her usual cheerful demeanor.

"Well, I have some volumes of poetry, but given that family home evening is so much a Latter-day Saint practice, I wonder if perhaps you would consider reading from the scriptures?"

Bel agreed that it would be entirely appropriate but, not knowing the scriptures herself, asked Mrs. Anderton to choose the passage. It had to be inspiring, thought-provoking, and interesting, something that would be understood by all and that would lend itself to the skill of recitation. It also had to be as beautifully worded as the poetry she would otherwise have chosen.

Mrs. Anderton took her battered leather scriptures from the bookcase and thumbed through them thoughtfully before passing the book over to Bel. "Mosiah, chapter two, begin at verse nine. You might like to read it all now but just select parts to read for this evening. It's a speech given by a wise king to his people, so it's perfect for declaring to a gathering such as ours."

Bel scanned the passage quickly and agreed that it more than fulfilled her requirements. Then she looked with interest at the cover of the book. "What exactly is this Book of Mormon?"

If Gwen had felt a little less distracted by what had passed between Edward and her earlier, she knew she would have been able to answer Bel's question with words given her by the Holy Spirit and with a gentleness and love she truly felt. But as she searched her mind and heart quickly, Gwen despaired that this good and honest young woman was looking for an introduction to the gospel of Jesus Christ from someone whose mind was too occupied elsewhere to focus on her needs or even to invite the Spirit in prayer. She answered by habit more than conviction. "It's a book of scripture brought forth in these latter days by a prophet of God. It stands alongside the Bible."

"There's one in my room," Bel remembered.

"Yes, yes, that's right. You might like to read the introduction. It tells you how important the Book of Mormon is. You can keep that copy, too. Take it home with you."

At the mention of home, Bel's face lost its expression of interest and became blank, her lips pressed firmly together. "Thanks. Look, I—I'd better go. We're all going out shopping together."

Gwen realized that the moment had passed and was lost. Bel was no longer thinking about the Book of Mormon but instead appeared to be distracted by another matter.

"Will you learn and recite it, or will you read it?" Gwen asked.

"I think I'd like to select a short section and recite it," Bel said cautiously. "I know I don't have long, but I'm quite good at memorizing, and it is so much more effective. Danny's doing a comedy spot, by the way. I think he'll be good, too."

Gwen nodded, but they had run out of things to say to one another, and Bel soon took her leave. Watching her join up with Danny, Steve and Jake, Gwen sighed as they left, relieved that there would be no more interruptions to her quiet thought, but sad at knowing that she had been only halfheartedly involved in the conversation. The Spirit had not been with her as she spoke to Bel; she had been too upset by her disagreement with Edward. As a result, she had served Bel very badly. She admitted with some trepidation that she needed to swallow her pride and speak to Edward, even apologize. Nothing could be right until she did.

❦

To Bel's great relief, Steve drove with greater care than he had the previous day, perhaps because he no longer felt the need to show off his driving ability to her or maybe because he had matured in her company. The music was quieter, too, and Bel almost enjoyed listening to it this time.

They drove to Porthmadog first, a busy bustling town where they discovered a superb delicatessen with rabbit, hare, and pheasants hanging upside down outside over racks of exotic vegetables, and all manner of beans and legumes set out in trays with scoops and polythene bags inside. There was an impressive array of cheeses, local and international, fresh herbs growing in pots, and ready-made patés in earthenware dishes laid out in rows. Steve seemed immediately inspired, and Bel was gratified that he asked her opinion and suggestions as he contemplated new ideas that would take advantage of the variety offered. They were nearly half an hour in the shop, and both Danny and Jake quickly became bored. Danny suggested that he and Jake go to a more interesting toy shop, and they left eagerly.

When they met later for fish and chips in a white-tiled restaurant, Jake proudly showed his mother the toy spaceship Danny had bought him, and Steve, just as smugly, indicated the two carrier bags filled to overflowing with his purchases.

In Criccieth they found a wholefoods shop that appeared to specialize in sauces and condiments, flavored chocolates and locally baked biscuits, and a fishmonger's shop, where they selected smoked salmon, fresh king prawns, oysters, and the samphire Steve had been so certain they would have to gather themselves from the marshes at Conwy.

It had been a successful outing, but the weather was warm, so Steve suggested they head back to Haven immediately to put the fish into the refrigerator. He wanted to get started on the preparation, and Danny and Bel had just as much to prepare. Danny had not yet scripted his act, and Bel had seven long verses to learn by heart.

Before leaving the town, Bel commented that it would be a pity not to go to see how the painter was getting on at the seafront, especially since Steve, Danny, and Jake all featured in the painting. The young men readily agreed that they could spare the time and were keen to see the picture, so once again they treated themselves to delicious creamy ices and basked in the sunshine as they strolled down to the promenade.

The painter was still there in the same place, frowning in concentration. Bel was a little worried at disturbing him, so they hovered some distance behind him. Sensing their presence, the painter turned warily, then smiled in recognition and invited them all over to look at his work.

"It's almost finished now and I'm quite pleased with it," he said quietly as they gazed appreciatively at the picture. He had used his artist's eye to bring out the sparkles in the sea, the life in the young men as they played with the dog on the glittering wet rocks and sand, the radiance of the sun as it pierced the thin clouds with warming silver shafts, and the colorful buckets, spades, and brightly clad sun worshippers that littered the beach. Above it all stood the deep gray brooding castle, solid and dull, as though it were the only reality surrounded by insubstantial dreams. It evoked a wonderful sense of permanence about the structure set against the transience of the modern landscape around it and Steve, who felt things deeply, was affected by the power of the picture and his small part in helping to create it.

"It's incredible," he said at last, and Danny, also seeing the painting for the first time, agreed.

"Thank you," smiled the artist. "I should finish it in a couple of hours, hopefully before the rain starts."

Bel cast a look at the sky, but although there were a few clouds, she could see no sign that rain might be due. "Will you be selling it?" she asked, not really knowing why when she could never afford to buy it.

"I haven't decided. I may. Why, would you be interested?"

Bel wished she could answer otherwise but declined sorrowfully. "What about you, Steve?" she asked him, since he seemed to have some disposable income, at least. He had a nice new car and had just bought copious quantities of the finest foods without thought to the price, hadn't he?

"I love it," Steve said. "But I don't think so. I don't have a fireplace to hang it above."

The artist seemed not to want to talk further, turning his attention back to his work. They thanked him again and headed back towards the car.

"He seems a very nice man," Bel said, smiling to herself. Over the last six years, the only men she had known well had been Marty and his brother, Paul. It had been good to discover, during these last few days, that there were good and kind men in the world, too.

"There is something rather sad about him, though," Steve said with a shrug. "Just something I felt about him. He seemed almost afraid of us, as if he's become very isolated from the world."

Danny agreed. "Sometimes it's the most tortured souls who are the most artistic. Just look at all the poets—Shelley was crazy, Sylvia Plath killed herself."

She had realized early on just how intelligent Danny was, but now she realized that Steve was also clever and deeply artistic, although his medium was food, not paint. Bel wondered whether Steve was a tortured and lonely soul, too, if beneath the boyish charm there was a pain too deep to contemplate, one that he covered up by adopting a false, carefree adolescent attitude. Outwardly he was like any other man his age, good-looking, well-built, well-dressed, but there was another aspect to his character which she wondered at now that she was growing to know him a little better.

Both these men were special and she cared deeply for them both already. Even though they might only be together for a few days, she had a feeling that they would help her to become a stronger woman. She wondered if they might even help her learn to trust again.

CHAPTER 16

E dward?" Gwen spoke his name quietly, tentatively, holding out the filled baguette that was his lunch as though it were a peace offering. His noble face, framed by its half-halo of white hair, was red with the exertion of weeding, and the overflowing refuse sack beside him was testament to his hard work as much as was the neatness of their garden, a little patch of order and cultivation against the wilderness of the mountainside.

He looked up and smiled with such delight at seeing her, that all the fears she had nursed and nurtured disappeared immediately. She knew that she loved him as deeply as ever, and they could and would work through whatever it was that had come between them that morning. He declined the baguette, protesting his dirty hands, and instead gathered up the refuse sack and his gardening tools, returned them to the shed, and then sought her out in the kitchen. His lunch now sat on a plate on the table, accompanied by a light salad.

"You're a wonderful woman, Gwen Anderton," Edward said, eyeing his plateful hungrily before pronouncing a brief blessing over the food.

She was reluctant to mention their disagreement this morning. Her relief that everything seemed normal again was so great that rather than face it and resolve it, she would rather forget that they had ever had such a hurtful difference of opinion. But it would nag and fester and grow, she knew, and already it seemed to have driven away some of the testimony she took for granted.

"Edward . . . ," she began hesitantly. "About what you said this morning—"

"I'm so sorry if I upset you or offended you," Edward blurted out, interrupting her in his relief that she was talking about it. "I really didn't mean to. You know I love you and I admire the way you do so much for your guests. It's just—" he paused and looked at her helplessly, "—I just felt that you shouldn't."

Her hurt gave way to intrigue. "Felt? In what way?"

He struggled for the words. "I think it may have been the Spirit, although I'm still learning how to recognize it. I just felt that Mr. McNaught needed to have the peace he had asked for and that you needed to leave him to himself. I don't know why I thought it or where it came from."

It had been barely a year since Edward had first begun to understand the workings of the Spirit in his life and the almost imperceptible but still recognizable answers from a heavenly source. Still, Gwen had difficulty at times remembering that she was no longer the only person in their home entitled to such spiritual guidance. She felt rather petulant for asking it, but had to know anyway. "Then why didn't I feel anything?"

He stared into space for a moment, deep in thought, but was unable to reach any conclusion. "I don't know. To be honest, I'm not as used to all this as you are, and I am still wondering why I feel it so strongly myself."

But Gwen understood suddenly that it might be as much a lesson for her as for her husband. A lesson in humility, in acceptance, in listening to her spouse and honoring him by valuing his opinions even when they differed from her own, lest they drive a wedge between them.

"Well, there is one way to find out for sure," she said, smiling at him.

Edward looked at her questioningly.

"We do what the Spirit directs and see what happens," she said, grateful for the peace which had come through understanding better what had prompted Edward's words this morning.

He smiled at her and reached out to squeeze her hand. "You're a wise woman. I'm very lucky to have you."

She smiled thoughtfully and when she was still quiet a few minutes later, he asked what she was thinking. "Just that marriage is harder than it looks."

He laughed at that, remembering just how hard it could really be and how wonderful it was to be married to Gwen.

⁕

Jake had little difficulty choosing what to do for the talent contest. For weeks he had been impressing his friends with his astonishingly accurate rendition of his favorite song from the latest Disney movie. He was not dissuaded by the possibility that few of his adult audience would even recognize the tune, and he sang it to his mother that afternoon in their room, accompanying it with the appropriate sound effects and spirited dancing. He accepted his mother's standing ovation, then settled down to scratching his name roughly on postcards to the same friends who had applauded his performance only last week, and whom he would probably never see again. Bel was not even sure that she wanted to post the cards, lest Marty find out and discover their whereabouts by the postmark. It was only a very small risk, though. They would be moving on soon anyway, and it would be nice for Jake.

She was being silly, she reasoned, being so afraid of Marty all the time. They were far away, quite safe, and he would not find her until she was ready. She returned her attention to the difficult task of learning the beautiful old language of the Book of Mormon. She had been studying it for almost an hour while Jake played outside with Steve, Danny, and Lucy, and she now almost had it. Pleased with her progress, she asked Danny to listen to her later that afternoon, and he confirmed that she was almost word perfect.

She smiled with satisfaction. "How's your act coming along?"

He shrugged. "I'm putting it together in my head as we speak. I suppose I won't know until I perform it tonight. I don't want to practice on you or you won't laugh tonight. I'll just take it as it comes, I think."

"I hope you don't mind my asking . . . ," she said slowly, with the long, drawn-out intonation of someone certain that she was overstepping her bounds, "but I've been wondering how it is that you're only a waiter? You're obviously very intelligent. Surely you could have had some high-flying, well-paid job somewhere?"

"I'm not so intelligent," he shrugged. "Just ordinary. I went to school like everyone else, found it boring but did well enough. Then I went to college but didn't think much of it. I'd been working in the hotel since I was fourteen, doing weddings on Saturdays, and helping out on some evenings, so when they offered me a full-time job, I took it."

Bel had always enjoyed learning at school and couldn't imagine being bored. "Why didn't you like college?" she asked.

He shrugged again. "Poor teachers, I suppose. I kept asking them questions about things they were supposed to know and they couldn't answer. I got frustrated with it all."

"I see," she said, starting to smile. "So you were too intelligent, too clever for your teachers."

He shrugged again. "I'm just a lifetime underachiever." He seemed unwilling to say anything more, and she thought it was likely that he didn't want to be different. He just wanted to be one of the lads and have fun while he was still young. Since a high IQ undoubtedly made him "different," Danny was probably embarrassed by it, though conscious of it and quick to draw upon it when it suited him. It explained a great deal about him, she thought.

They were in the lounge again, each seated on one of those wonderfully deep and comfortable straight-backed armchairs that offered a superb view of the valley through the narrow windows. The stone walls were thick and the glass in the windows was leaded. She felt as though she were in a castle, her own secret fortress against the world. This room was her favorite place now; she felt safe here, secure and happy.

It was astonishing how quickly and easily she had found the protection she had sought, she mused. Everything about Haven was perfect, from its location to the people to be found within its walls. They were a family, she decided, not just she and Jake but Danny and Steve, too, and the Andertons, and perhaps even that family with the three small children. A "family home evening" seemed entirely appropriate.

Both she and Danny had been silent, lost in their thoughts. Then Danny spoke up. "Well, if I'm so intelligent, perhaps you'll forgive me if I use my brain. You're running away from something—or someone—aren't you?"

Danny's question caught her by surprise, coming as it did from out of the blue. She stared blankly at him, conscious that the answer was evident in her cautious expression. "How did you know?"

"Oh, your behavior, body language, a few things Jake said, and some things that didn't seem quite right. How you acted about Jake this morning. Gwen had a word with me about it afterwards; I gather you went to pieces." He paused and Bel flushed, acknowledging that this had been the case.

"And then there's that little band of white skin around your ring finger," he said slowly and deliberately. "You've been out in the sun with a wedding ring on, and you've only recently taken it off. You didn't answer when I asked where you came from and how long you planned on staying here. I think you left your husband. I don't think he was physically abusive—you don't seem to have any scars or bruises—but judging from your nervousness and lack of confidence, and the fact that you are totally thrown for a loop by a simple compliment, I suspect he was verbally cruel to you, and probably to the boy as well."

She sighed. "Danny, you're right, but I really don't want to say any more about it. It's been difficult and I'm not entirely ready to trust anyone quite yet. I'm still afraid he's going to come after us."

She was a little disconcerted to see an expression that looked like triumph cross Danny's face, and he turned away from her as though their conversation was over. Startled, she wondered whether he might be too immature to contemplate such troubles as hers, whether he wished to end their conversation now that she had confirmed his hypothesis. "I'm sorry, you don't need to be hearing this."

He swallowed, seemed unable to look at her, and she was yet more surprised to see that his usual mask of confident assurance had slipped, he seemed troubled now, shaking his head as though confused and pressing his hands together. When he did speak again, it was with hesitation. "I—Is there anything I can do to help? I mean, what happens next? Where will you go when you leave Haven?"

An excellent question, Bel reflected, for even she did not really know the answer. "I'm going to look for a job. Something part time that will fit in with school hours. Jake is due to start school soon, and I hope I'll have found something by then and can enroll him at the local school. I'll rent a little flat somewhere. I have some savings that should last until I can find something. But as for *where*—" she shrugged, "—that depends on where the jobs are."

"In Ireland," he said casually, as though it were not a bombshell. He seemed to be recovering his usual equanimity.

"Ireland?" she repeated, stunned at the suggestion and what it might imply.

"Have you ever thought of waitressing? There are always vacancies for staff. It's harder than it looks, the money is terrible and you don't get a lot of respect, but you'd have no problems getting a job at our hotel even without experience, especially if I put in a good word for you. They have live-in, too, so you'd be perfectly set up. And there's a good school within walking distance so you could get rid of that rusty old roller-skate you call a car."

"Ireland," she said again, knowing from his expression that Danny was patiently waiting for it to sink into her slow mind. She was irritated to look so foolish in front of him.

"You know, across the sea, the emerald isle—"

"Thank you. I do know where it is," she said. She heard the edge in her voice and knew it was because she had been so surprised at the suggestion. Knowing that Wales was another country from her own, she had felt that a border of sorts between Marty and her was somehow symbolically important, but a sea and passport control offered even more protection. It was perfect. Ireland was beautiful, she had always heard, but— She shook her head. "I can't take Jake to Ireland. It would be tantamount to kidnapping him."

"Fine, right, well, it was just a thought." He was as quickly and easily dismissive of the idea as he had been in suggesting it, and she felt deflated and rejected to see how little the proposal had meant to him. For a moment she had hoped that he might actually want her company, that he might be suggesting he would be disappointed when they parted in a few days' time. It had been a good feeling, one that had swelled in her a strange hope and pride and affection for him.

Now she was left wondering exactly who Danny O'Hanlon was. Was he an immature young lad who thought of nothing but larking around and having a good time, or was he an intelligent, sensitive man who understood her and was beginning to care for her. She hoped she might find out before they parted forever.

CHAPTER 17

E dward gave the prayer that began family home evening, marveling at how willingly this odd assortment of people bowed their heads, with the exception of Angela. Peering at her for the briefest moment as he asked blessings on them all, he noticed that she was looking resolutely ahead and seemed not to be listening. He remembered the first family home evening he and his first wife, Edith, had attended at Haven. She had objected to everything that was said and done, demanding to know what right anyone had to tell her how to live her life, and Edward had suggested that they stay away in future. But he knew that was just her way and that she had probably enjoyed the evening as much as anything she had ever done.

As guests at Haven, they had attended the following year as well, and again Edith had taken issue with the points raised. Gwen had never taken offense, rather she made it clear that Edith had a right to her opinion and a right to voice it. She even went so far as to say that stimulating discussion could be beneficial at times, but even so, Edward had been deeply embarrassed. Family home evening at Haven had been far more pleasant since Edith had passed on, especially those treasured times he remembered when the other guests had declined their invitations to attend and it had been just Gwen and himself studying together.

Although Danny O'Hanlon had the unenviable task of presenting his talent first, he could not have looked more engaging. He wore the same casual trousers, loose shirt, and charming smile as he had that morning when Bel had enjoyed speaking to him so much. His dark eyes sparkled with mischief, and he presented himself before his audience with a confidence that spoke of his trust in them as much as of his own outgoing nature. He said nothing for a moment and they all assumed he was collecting his thoughts. A few more seconds went by, and the others began to cast glances around as they looked for an explanation for his silence. His eyes remained fixed on the audience, studying them one by one, waiting for the nervous giggles that Bel dutifully but involuntarily offered.

"I'm a mime," Danny announced at last in a loud voice which broke the strained silence and made Jake jump. "It's just I'm a terrible actor." The first tentative laughs broke out. "That's the problem, you see. I'm not much good at anything now.

"It's my age, you know. Really. You know you're getting past it when you and your mother start approaching the same age from opposite ends. It's not that I'm over the hill exactly—let's just say I've got a good view of the valley." There was more appreciative laughter, especially from Gwen and Edward.

"That's the problem with getting old. Everything starts to go. I've put on a lot of weight. You wouldn't know it to look at me, but I used to be seven pounds nine ounces. I was thinking of getting some surgery, you know, liposuction, tummy tuck, a face lift. In fact, I lost a lot of money that way once. I loaned a friend a thousand pounds for some plastic surgery, and now I can't get it back because I don't know what he looks like." Even Angela couldn't help smiling at this one.

"I had another friend had his face lifted. Well, you can't leave anything lying around these days." A shout of laughter from Steve here. "He kept going back and going back, getting this improved and that tweaked, but it did no good. In the end I just had to tell him he looked ridiculous. That wiped the smile off the back of his neck, I can tell you." More laughter, and a guffaw from Stuart Kirby.

Bel found all her expectations of Danny's performance matched and exceeded as she giggled at his deadpan delivery, his casual and slightly bored expression, and his quick speech with that wonderful, quirky accent. Around her she saw the other guests were equally helpless with mirth. Mr. Anderton had dissolved into chuckles at Danny's first suggestion that he was old at twenty-four, and as Danny's wit turned to other subjects of interest to his audience, and his wry observations rang hilariously true, each in turn found themselves laughing aloud with him and at him. When he had finished, they clapped until their hands were sore, but Danny just sauntered back to his corner and sat cross-legged on the floor. He seemed oblivious to them all, but Bel, who knew him best of anyone except Steve perhaps, caught his eye just for a second and could tell that he was pleased with his success.

Jake followed, aware even at his tender age that he wasn't likely to compare well with such an impressive performance. Still, the bold singing of the spirited child moved many of the listeners, and he, too, was applauded loudly.

Gwen followed the young boy's act, bringing out a large sewing basket from which she took some beautifully crafted and colorful samplers and exquisite pictures worked in tiny cross-stitch. Her family tree, taken down from its place on the wall but still in its gold frame, had been worked in this manner with names embroidered in a calligraphic stitch linked with fine silver threads and decorated with swirls of color and little flowers. Half completed was a sampler recording her marriage to Edward Anderton. The intricate border was finished as were their names. Below these, in deep blue thread, were the words "Sealed for time and all eternity in the Salt Lake Temple . . ." and then it was blank. Gwen explained that she thought it best not to complete this part until it had actually happened.

Her fine work was much admired, although Angela said nothing. Both she and Stuart had declined to perform, and although Danny's wit had brought a smile to her face, she made it clear that she was there by coercion. She sat on one of the straight-backed dining room chairs in the farthest corner, holding two-year-old Adam on her lap like a barrier. Gwen imagined that at the earliest opportunity, once she felt her debt to her father was repaid, she would excuse herself by protesting the children's bedtime. And since it was already seven-thirty, she would be justified in doing so.

Bel was the next to stand, and choosing a position in the very center of the room, she waited for complete silence before drawing a deep breath. She allowed her gentle voice to resonate with a mellow tone as she declared the words of King Benjamin, and her skillful recitation gave them a strength, grace, and emotion that bound her audience just as that original greater congregation of Nephites must have been enraptured. The poetry and deep truths of the words struck deep as Bel recited them with care and feeling, unafraid to meet the eyes of each listener. All were moved to deep thought and reflection as they listened, and Gwen found tears in her eyes as the familiar words took on a new dimension, and she was not ashamed to let them fall.

Bel concluded by telling her audience, in her natural voice, though with a reverent tone, the source of the words she had recited. She went on to say, "This book is believed to be holy scripture by our hosts, Mr. and Mrs. Anderton, and having read and learned just this part, I can say that I too believe it to hold many wonderful and inspiring truths, and wise guidance, and will try to read further." She sat down and Gwen smiled, overwhelmed that something she had said, even when she had not felt the Spirit giving her those words, had at least reached Bel. She prayed silently there and then that the young woman's reading of the book would bear a sweet fruit.

All the talents that were to be exhibited during that part of the evening had been shared, and Edward stood up to give a brief lesson. He spoke slowly and in simple terms, explaining that every person there, even those who had not chosen to demonstrate them, had talents and fine qualities unique to themselves. He told them that every child of God was different, equipped with the abilities each needed to overcome their personal trials and achieve their own potential. They were all loved and valued by a Heavenly Father, who knew their strengths and wanted to increase their measure daily, and who also knew their weaknesses and wanted to help them overcome them. No one present found any objection to what he said. He phrased his speech with certainty and delicacy, and delivered the words in a loving manner with a smile that encompassed them all. Gwen was to offer the closing prayer, but before she did so she took Edward's hand without embarrassment and said, "I think my husband has shown his talent this evening, too. He gave a superb talk in church yesterday, and he has demonstrated here how eloquently he can speak and how well he can put matters into words that everyone can understand and so easily convey things that speak to our hearts."

Edward hardly heard the prayer she offered next. He was thinking with delight and some pride about Gwen's faith in him and appreciation of him, wondering if she might be right that he was perhaps an able and gifted public speaker. President Chugg had also complimented him on his talk, and he thought of the attentive faces of the guests in the lounge that evening as they had listened to him, sometimes nodding almost imperceptibly in agreement, often returning his smile. Did he really have this gift? He had never had cause to think about talents until today when Gwen suggested he give the lesson after the evening's demonstrations, and it had not occurred to him to look for his own talent. Yet now he seemed to have discovered it purely by chance. Suffused with happiness as he listened to Gwen give thanks for the diverse capabilities of the assembled friends, he reflected that membership in the Church of Jesus Christ had not only given him hope and understanding but a lovely wife and the opportunity to discover himself in ways he had never dreamed possible.

CHAPTER 18

S teve brought out his offerings as soon as the prayer was
finished. He was assisted by Danny, who carried three white
china plates at once, which held tiny canapés of strips of
smoked salmon delicately wound around sprigs of samphire, carefully
poised oysters and prunes wrapped in juicy bacon, forming traditional angels and devils on horseback, crisp aromatic prawn toasts,
and crumbly blue cheese tartlets. Steve followed behind with petit
fours and tiny pastries oozing with honey, cream, and nuts. The
hungry faces that watched them in contented wonderment proved
that Steve's talent was appreciated as much as any of the others had
been, and he was soon in demand for tips and recipes, not the least
for the mixed fruit punch he had blended to accompany the food. It
was a cheerful scene, and even Angela seemed to have forgotten all
her objections to being present as she chatted with Steve about the
growing popularity of vegetarianism.

Bel was the first to realize that their happy gathering was being
watched, and looking toward the stairs, she saw a tall man staring
down in puzzlement at them from the small gallery. She realized that
he must be the elusive guest whose car was parked outside but whose
table in the dining room had yet to be occupied, but his lean face and
gray hair were familiar and she felt certain she should know him from
elsewhere. It took a moment for her to recognize him as the artist

from the beach, and when she did, she smiled warmly at him. "Hello there! Did you finish the painting, then?" she asked, standing up and approaching the stairs.

"Yes, I did," he said, looking a little embarrassed.

"Then why don't you bring it down here for us to see? We're having a talent night, and you are certainly talented. What a marvelous coincidence that you're staying in the same guest house!"

The artist reddened slightly, but Bel's enthusiasm would not be thwarted, and she followed him into his room to bring out the painting and his sketch book.

Gwen had followed Bel's gaze and had been pleased to see that Brian McNaught had emerged from his room, presumably to discover the cause of all the noise and laughter which had disturbed his precious peace. She was just wondering what she might say to greet him and invite him to join them when Bel had thankfully taken it upon herself to befriend him. Gwen had gathered that Bel had met him already, but not knowing in what capacity, she was astonished when Bel walked triumphantly back in the lounge, Brian at her side and a large, unframed painting held up for all to see.

It was as beautiful in its intricate detail as it was in the message of transitory time it conveyed through its color and composition. Each brush stroke was used to extreme effect, from the lively flecks on the surf to the diluted grays of the castle stones. An awed silence was followed by murmurs of admiration, respect, and congratulation towards the artist, who did not seem to want to say much, but merely stood shyly beside Bel as though she were his spokesperson.

Gwen congratulated Mr. McNaught on his rare talent as she realized that the mysterious objects in his car must be his easel, paints, and other equipment. No wonder he had been out all day and insisted on peace. His very soul seemed to have gone into this exquisite work. Thank goodness she had listened to Edward and not attempted to press the man further.

The sketch book was passed around and admired by all with gasps of genuine wonder that such realistic representations could be created with just a few strokes of a pencil in so little time. Embarrassed at being the center of attention, Brian McNaught apologized that he had not brought any of his other paintings with him. He had not expected to meet anyone who might be interested, he said humbly, but then seemed to wish he had not spoken at all when he was inundated by the eager affirmations that flew at him as everyone insisted that his painting and sketches were wonderful and that he had a rare talent indeed. While the guests returned to their comfortable chairs, murmuring enthusiastically amongst themselves, Brian McNaught nervously took a seat and stared at the floor as Edward commented that the most impressive talent demonstrated that night had been the last.

"Do you do this for a living?" Angela asked, interested despite herself.

"No, no," he coughed, looking up uncomfortably. "I'm a lawyer—was. I'm, er, taking some time off."

"I'm so sorry I didn't tell you about family home evening or invite you," Gwen said, chagrined that she had feared his rudeness enough to exclude him. "I didn't think you'd want to come." It had been a terrible omission and Gwen was ashamed of herself now.

"I wouldn't have come," he replied simply, his offhand tone dismissing her apology as one not required. Then it had been for the best that she had said nothing to him, Gwen reflected. Had he known about the evening's entertainment, he would have locked himself in his room all night. This way his curiosity had brought him among them, into the family that was Haven, and he actually seemed to glean some pleasure from being part of their gathering despite his evident awkwardness.

"Will you be requiring breakfast in your room as usual tomorrow?" she asked quietly after a decent interval, and after ensuring the other guests were deep in conversation.

Brian hesitated thoughtfully before answering, "No, I think I'll come down to the dining room tomorrow. These seem to be nice people."

He had seemed rude, inexplicable, and secretive, Gwen acknowledged, embarrassed. His impoliteness had upset her and his forcibly voiced desire for privacy had irked her. Now she saw that he was chronically shy, since each time he spoke he reddened, shifted uncomfortably in his seat, and folded his arms tightly across his body. She saw that he disliked crowds, and while it was difficult for Gwen, who was naturally friendly and gregarious, to understand, she wondered whether there was something in his past which had led him to fear others.

Whatever it was, she guessed that he just wanted to forget it all this week, and to experience peace and solitude somewhere far from home. She could imagine that seclusion helped his artistic muse, and she should not have judged him so quickly for requiring it. Once again she was thankful for her husband's perspective and ashamed of herself for being too full of her own notions of friendliness and fellowship to see when someone needed solitude and space instead of solicitude.

⚜

Angela and her family went up to bed first, although they stayed far longer than Gwen had expected them to. Brian McNaught did not stay downstairs long either, seeming strained after only half an hour at having to make polite small talk with people he did not really know. When Edward and Gwen busied themselves clearing everything away, Bel rose to her feet and pulled Jake to his feet, ready to retire to their room. For once the child seemed ready for bed, for he yawned and complied without objection. As Bel stood, however, she was startled as a warm, strong hand slipped into hers. It was Danny, pulling her back to her seat.

"You've forgotten about *Frontier,*" he reminded her.

"I—I was going to watch it in our room," she replied, feeling awkward at the strange but electrifying feel of his hand on hers.

"No way, Mum! It's rubbish!" Jake protested, and Bel laughed at her son.

"Stay down here and watch it with me." Danny's voice was soft, insistent, and strangely hypnotic, his lazy brown eyes fixed fearlessly on hers.

Bel said nothing for a moment. It would certainly be easier to watch her favorite show down here than upstairs with Jake, who really should be asleep at such a late hour and probably would be but for the noise and brightness of the television.

It was not a difficult decision to make. "I'll put this urchin to bed and come back down when he's settled," she said, prompting Jake to say goodnight to Danny and Steve before they hurried upstairs together. As she reached the top step, she looked back on the cozy room below her, just in time to see Steve frown at his friend in apparent irritation. Danny returned the look with a self-satisfied smile of triumph and winked slyly. Steve sighed, muttered something which Bel couldn't quite catch, then called his dog and left with the Labrador through the front door.

Tired and comfortable, Jake nodded off during his bedtime story. Bel kissed him gently, then went back downstairs and settled beside Danny on the sofa, happy to see that the television was already on and the theme music from the show already playing. Danny's hand touched hers again, but held it more loosely, casually now. His warmth next to her made her feel strangely content and his presence drove out all thought of the fears which had plagued her, as though this young man might defend her against the evil that haunted her. As the dramatic unearthly images played across the television screen, and she saw Danny's excited grin, she wondered how it was that she could be so entirely happy only three days after leaving behind such terrible sorrow.

CHAPTER 19

Brian paused as he descended the stairs the next morning, partly to take a slow, deep breath in the manner he had been taught when he needed to calm himself, but also to survey the room he was entering before it filled with lively, noisy, frightening people.

The room looked peaceful, spacious and open with its outside wall of bare stone, a large original inglenook fireplace set into the far gable, and the inner wall adorned with a bookcase that reached to the ceiling. The assorted pictures arrayed across the flat walls showed very little blank space between them. There were framed prints of fine paintings of biblical scenes, a photograph of a religious building standing regally amid beautiful flower-filled grounds, a hand-stitched family tree, and a host of ancient black and white photographs along with several more modern ones. Against the fourth wall was the staircase on which he now stood. The room was well furnished with three deep and comfortable armchairs and a long settee, a magazine rack and small coffee table, and an old piano in a far corner. The front door opened directly into this lounge.

At a quarter to eight, Brian had hoped that he would be the first person to arrive downstairs and also that the next people to join him might be those he knew and felt able to talk to. In this he was fortunate, as Bel and Jake trotted down the stairs only a few minutes later and said their good mornings cheerfully. Bel chatted brightly about the possible change in the weather as she sat opposite him. He had been about to tell her, with some trepidation and apology, that he would be painting nearby that day when the front door burst open, making him start nervously. The two young Irish men appeared in the front door with their muddy and panting dog, all full of life, noisy, and active, but Brian did not feel as intimidated as he might by others of their vigor, for he found that he liked them and almost felt he knew them. They certainly meant him no harm and made no demands on him. And as they saw him sitting peaceably by the window, they even greeted him warmly, as though greeting one of their own.

The family, the only guests he felt a bit wary of, since they had spoken little the previous night, did not appear until after Mrs. Anderton had opened the dining room door to invite her guests to take their places for breakfast. Brian found that the meal was made even more delicious by the attractiveness of the room and the interesting chatter he could hear around him, none of which, so far as he could make out, related to him.

After breakfast Brian nodded to the Andertons and his fellow guests in what he hoped was a polite parting gesture, before hurrying back to the sanctuary of his room. There he washed his face again, splashing it with cold water this time, brushed his teeth, and filled his plastic lemonade bottles with water, and his thermos with tea. He escaped the house without the trauma of talking to anyone else and went to his car for his artist's tools.

His easel had originally been in a zip-up case, but that had torn long ago. He had to manhandle it awkwardly to his selected spot a few hundred yards up the mountain path from Haven and then return for everything else he would need. Edward, who was outside washing the windows when he returned, saw Brian grappling with the case that held his paints, his folding seat, and the carrier bag containing his thermos, sandwiches, and water, and was quickly beside him, offering to help. Brian's first instinct was to refuse the offer, but he stopped himself, reasoning that his host meant well and it would save him another trip. With the older man's assistance, Brian returned to the place where his easel now stood, another clean sheet of heavy textured paper already stretched onto it and held with masking tape.

"What a wonderful view," Edward said, observing the subject of Brian's next work as though it were the first time he was seeing it and not the sight he awoke to every morning. Placing the carrier bag at the foot of the easel, Edward stood for a moment admiring the beautiful and powerful glacial valley with its deep lake and the ancient stone tower strategically positioned on its banks, guarding the entrance to that secret enclave. In the foreground but set off to one side was Haven, the dark gray slate of its roof the same as that visible in the heaps cast up from the mines just across the mountain range.

"I hope I can do it justice," Brian said, and it was not mere modesty but a genuine fear that his ability was not great enough to be entrusted with such an awesome task as recreating this scene. He thanked his host for his trouble, pleased to see that the man, understanding that Brian wanted peace to work, had set off back down the mountain to continue cleaning the windows.

Brian found that he liked the Andertons. They seemed to be good people. But that didn't mean he wanted to be drawn into conversation with them, or with anyone else for that matter, even the gentle, delicate young woman he had first met on the beach. It was all just too much. Alone here on the mountain, he was safe with only the sheep, his easel, and his thoughts for company. People were too difficult, too complex; they had begun to terrify him, and he wished he could shut himself away from them forever. But for all that, he knew he was getting better, and that week, for the first time in months, the world had started to look like somewhere he might want to live.

He remembered the day, barely a week ago, when he had looked into his wife's pale face as he stood on the welcome mat at their front door. She had said nothing, merely folded her arms tightly, pressing them into her stomach. She had met his gaze with mustered pride and reddened eyes, her teeth pressed together to prevent her chin from shaking, as it always did when she cried. He knew that she was afraid to let him go. Over the last year, the fierce mothering instinct in her had taken hold as she had seen his terror. She held him when he felt wretched, encouraged him when he could see no sign of hope, and assured him that she could not bear to be without him when he told her how much better things would be if he were not there.

She had always been there for him. As a small boy he had slipped in an icy puddle on the school playground and fallen, cutting his knee badly. Through his tears, he had seen a stocky girl with short black hair regarding him with compassion, her face screwed up as though she could feel his pain. She helped him limp to the school nurse, who had dabbed something that stung horribly on the wound, and then stuck a huge plaster over his knee so that there was barely any skin visible between where his short trousers ended and his long socks began.

The girl had watched, her head tipped to one side, fascinated, but had not said a word until the nurse had asked what she was still doing there.

"Can I have two of those?" she had asked. "My knees are cold."

She was chased away for her cheek, but Brian had admired her from that day on. He learned that her name was Fiona and that she lived not far from his house. She was studious and thoughtful, she didn't say much, and she didn't care about being popular. When he was fifteen, he finally plucked up enough courage to send her an anonymous valentine. She had confronted him at school, asking whether it had been from him, and Brian, knowing that his reddened cheeks gave him away, had confessed.

"Good," she said. "I've been wanting to see the new James Bond film. Would you take me?"

They had married the year he qualified as a solicitor and raised their two children in quiet contentment. She trained as a nurse, and he was continually astonished at her considerable inner strength and determination. She dealt daily, and often nightly, with disasters and emergencies that claimed precious lives, and then came home and smiled as brightly as when she had left for her shift. All the while Brian found it increasingly difficult to get through the piles of work on his desk, as he grew more irritated and angry at the interruptions of clients and phone calls. He began working later and later, pushing aside the nagging feelings of frustration and futility.

Sometimes he would come into his office, grunt at his bored secretary, and just stare at his desk, marveling at his own insanity in ever thinking he might be able to undertake the work ahead of him. Occasionally he might dare to reach out and shuffle through some papers, wondering where he could start without neglecting something yet more pressing. He felt his spine and shoulders cramping up the moment he sat in his leather swivel chair, and he bitterly hated everything in that room. Especially himself.

Everything seemed to be urgent these days; no one was prepared to wait anymore. But he was only one man and he could not do everything. Lately he wondered whether he could do anything. Yet the bills and demands kept arriving, and his clients, entirely confident in his abilities and unaware of the inadequacy he saw in himself, kept asking him to do more and more. For years he had tried to keep all the balls in the air, until a year ago everything had come crashing down. After he had gruffly sent her home one day, his secretary had called his wife, and Fiona had arrived to find him, seated in his leather chair, now shoved to the far corner of the room. His head was back against the wall and tears were coursing down his face.

He had clutched at Fiona, muttering that this was the end, he couldn't cope any more. He had not worked since that black and horrible day. His doctor had diagnosed him with severe stress-related depression, and Fiona had stopped work in order to care for him, their health insurance mercifully allowing her to do so. Brian wondered why she bothered; he was worse than a child. There seemed no reason for anything anymore; there was just an empty nothing that stretched ahead as far as he dared to look. He dragged himself from his bed each morning and, without really caring what he wore, he forced himself to dress. In the bathroom, he stared at the sink, willing himself to turn on the tap and wash his face or brush his teeth. Such simple tasks seemed insurmountable obstacles to be overcome.

Worst of all was the fear. Torn at every moment by terrible anxieties, he feared everyone. He was confused by people, didn't understand them, and refused to see them, and yet he was terrified to be alone with his dark thoughts. He was petrified at the thought that Fiona might leave him, and yet he forced himself to face it, to admit that it would be for the best. He knew he was worse than worthless to her. He was a burden, a pathetic excuse for a man; every man she passed in the street could offer her more than he could. He wondered why she stayed with him. For a time he wondered whether it might be out of pity, and he was as distressed at that likelihood as he was convinced by it. He was deliberately rude and unpleasant to her, hoping that his attitude might help her overcome her misplaced charity and finally leave.

Late one evening as he lay staring at the ceiling from the relative safety of his side of the bed, he brusquely told his wife that she was too fat. Actually, Fiona was exactly as he wanted her to be, but he despaired at how burdensome she must find the obligation of sleeping beside him. He knew that she was sensitive about her weight; perhaps it would give her the push she needed to leave, to go on, to build a new life with a man who could appreciate her, provide for her properly, and make her happy.

She was silent for a moment and then said, "I'll try to lose a bit of weight, then, if it'd please you." He'd grunted in reply, rolled onto his side, away from her, and pretended to drift off to sleep. He always pretended to her that he was sleeping, although sometimes it took him hours to do so.

He felt Fiona lying quietly beside him for five minutes before her body jerked. A sob escaped her then, and she gave way to pitiable crying, which left him, still pretending to be asleep, feeling even more wretched than before. At breakfast the next morning, he watched her forego her croissant with jam in favor of a meager half grapefruit and realized that unlikely as it seemed, she must love him after all. He still felt black and empty inside, but that first whisper of comfort from her sacrifice—for him—might have been the start of his recovery.

CHAPTER 20

I'm sorry it won't be very interesting for you," she began, "but I'll buy you an ice cream afterwards—"

"I won't go!" Even bribery was no match for Jake's determination not to go to whatever dull place his mother wanted to take him. He was standing only a few yards from the front door, his jacket in a heap at his feet where he had thrown it.

"We're going climbing," Danny put in lazily, not looking up from his book. "He can come with us if he wants to."

Gwen entered the lounge as Bel shot Danny a disbelieving stare and said, "I don't think so. Thanks anyway." Bel wondered what sort of mother they thought she was, allowing a small child to take part in a dangerous activity, especially in such reckless company.

"He could stay here with us," Gwen said, and this comment was altogether more welcome.

Bel turned to her gratefully. "Really, do you mean that?"

"Of course. We've no plans for the day; we'd enjoy his company. We've got plenty of toys here for him to play with. I don't suppose Peter will mind sharing them."

"Please, Mum, can I? I don't want to go to the job centers. Can I stay here?"

It was an ideal solution and Bel had not been looking forward to trying to entertain a bored child at the same time as scanning job advertisements. She seized the offer with gratitude, kissed her son good-bye, and smiled as Gwen took Jake back to the kitchen to help her bake a cake, wondering whether this culinary chore had originally been part of Gwen's plan for the day or whether she knew that all children loved cooking.

"Hey, Bel!" Steve called as he descended the stairs, dressed in his tight-fitting climbing gear. "Would you like to come out for a drink with us tonight?"

Danny looked up when he heard his friend and smiled to confirm that he approved the invitation. The thought of a night out in adult company, and with such special friends, too, was very tempting. Still, Bel was reluctant.

"I'd need to ask Mrs. Anderton to babysit for Jake again . . ."

"We'd be delighted," Mr. Anderton said from behind his newspaper at his favorite place in the corner of the lounge. Bel had forgotten he was there.

"Well, who's driving?" Bel asked, looking from Danny, to Steve, and back to Danny, who shrugged. Neither seemed keen to volunteer, since it would mean staying off the alcohol. She was similarly unenthusiastic about the prospect of enduring Steve's crazy driving and quickly said, "I don't drink so I'll do the driving if you like."

"Excellent idea to invite a driver, Steve. Great stuff!" and Danny laughed his delightful laugh. Bel could not help but join in, already excited to spend time in the company of friends and hopeful that she might soon find a good job, somewhere to live, and a new life to lead. She might even have something to celebrate with them tonight.

When they had baked the cake and licked the delicious sweet remnants from the mixing bowl, Gwen and Jake washed their hands thoroughly and then made sandwiches together for lunch. Mr. Anderton said grace, which Jake found very curious, having never imagined it might be necessary before hearing one the previous evening, then they ate in the lounge balancing their plates on their laps. The sandwiches were delicious, with their soft fresh bread, creamy cheese, and thick ham, and Jake told Mrs. Anderton how much he liked the food she cooked and was looking forward to tasting the cake that even now was baking in the oven.

Gwen was delighted with the compliment and smiled warmly. Children spoke so honestly and readily, and Jake's presence was refreshing and invigorating. For the first time, she began to think about what she had missed by marrying so late in life and never having children of her own.

She had done the right thing, she knew, in waiting for the right man, one who shared her values and faith. Edward was all she had ever dreamed of, and apart from their recent slight disagreement, their courtship and marriage had been wonderful, based on mutual and frequently expressed love, tenderness, and respect. Through him, she now had three lovely grandchildren. She wished she might spend more time with them, get to know them for themselves, but she knew Angela's heart was hardened against her and contact with her grandchildren would not be possible until her stepdaughter felt otherwise. She pulled herself back to the moment lest she become dejected.

"Come along, Jake. Run and get your jacket. Edward will get the cake out to cool while we're out," she said as she took his empty plate away.

"Where are we going?"

"Well, Mr. McNaught, who you saw last night, is painting a lovely picture of Haven and of the countryside. Would you like to come for a little walk and see it? Then later you could do some painting yourself. I've got a lovely box of watercolors somewhere."

Jake loved painting and, excited at the idea, he rushed upstairs to get his jacket as fast as he could. Soon he was running up the familiar mountain path to where the artist sat oblivious to everything but the view and the paint on his brushes. Jake wished Lucy was there to play with, but she had gone rock climbing with her master. He wondered if Steve and Danny took her up the cliff with them or if they tied her up somewhere.

Gwen had never looked after a child for so long and was finding it an exhilarating and satisfying experience, although she hoped Jake would allow her a few minutes to chat with Brian McNaught before he tore off up the mountain again. Fortunately, the little boy seemed impressed by the painting; his eyes opened wide as he saw the easel, and he said something to Mr. McNaught, which brought a humble smile to the man's face. As Gwen caught up and saw the elegantly sketched soft lines of the mountains and the first splash of color bringing a translucence into the lake, she understood why Jake admired it and added her compliments to his. Brian McNaught blushed and explained that the mountains had an unusual tone that he was struggling with, something about not having the usual purple base. Gwen nodded and pretended she understood about art, but really she only knew that it promised to be a superb picture.

"You know, you should try to do this for a living, Mr. McNaught. Your talent would be wasted if you didn't spend more time painting, and I'm sure you could sell them for a good deal of money."

"It is what I want to do more than anything," he acknowledged with some reserve.

"Then why don't you?"

"I've got two children at University. Their tuition is free, of course, but we're still expected to contribute to their living expenses. Practicing law brings in good money. I'm afraid it would be too much of a risk to give that up altogether for something that might never earn me a penny."

"But you told me yesterday that you're taking some time off work. Why don't you spend that time painting, and see whether you can exhibit or sell them? If you can sell your work, then you'll know that you don't need to go back to being a solicitor."

He smiled shyly. "I had thought of that. Painting is my first love really. I find it so restful. I'm off work because I—er, well I had been suffering with stress, and I had a bit of a breakdown a few months ago. I'm getting better now. Having this time to myself has helped tremendously."

Jake had started running back up the track but was not going far, just looking for somewhere he could get an even better view of the valley. Gwen felt profound pity for Brian as she understood why he had seemed so rude and had demanded to be left alone. She still wanted to help him if she could, now that he had managed to open up to her, and she was glad that Jake was not demanding her attention for the moment.

"When are you going back to work?"

"I've got six months off altogether. I've taken three of those already."

"Then you've got three more months to paint. I'd certainly be interested in buying this one when it's finished, if you'll name your price. And if you're looking for more interesting landscapes, I have some friends in Yorkshire with a lovely bed and breakfast in a very scenic area. I'm sure they'd give you a good rate if I asked them."

"That's very kind of you." As his brush gently dabbed a gray wash over the farthest mountain, he added, his voice low, "I should thank you, too, for letting me have the peace I needed. I really didn't want to mix too much with people. I'm a bit off in social matters, to be honest. I'm not very good at talking. You brought my meals to my room and you didn't pry or try to get me to talk. I must have seemed very strange to you. Thank you for respecting my wishes. This is a very peaceful place. It's what I needed."

It was the most she had ever heard him say, and the effort of speaking to her must have been very great, for he was pale and his eyes remained focused on the view before him and his painting, as though to meet her eyes would be too much for him. Now he was ready to eat in the dining room, to exchange a few words with the other guests, and to tell Gwen about himself, whereas two days ago he had been afraid to even be in this strange place among such lively and unfamiliar people. Although Gwen was finding it difficult to curb her naturally friendly and curious personality, she resolved to give him the space and peace he needed. Brian McNaught needed time alone to heal, and that was perhaps the greatest gift she could give him.

CHAPTER 21

Gwen had bought a beautiful box of watercolor paints and some thick paper in rainbow colors in preparation for the visit from her new grandchildren, and while it was good to see Jake enjoying them, she felt a little wistful realizing that she had spent only a few minutes with Peter, Adam, and Rosie since their arrival. She would have loved to hold the baby just for a minute, but as tired as Angela must be, she was even more resentful. There seemed to be no way to soften her heart.

But Gwen was not one to despair. Whenever anything troubled her, she would pray about it and then try to forget the matter, trusting that it had been committed to the loving hands of her Father. All the same, as she sat beside Jake at the kitchen table and watched him push the brush across the sodden paper, imagining himself to be creating a masterpiece to rival Brian McNaught's, she felt particularly despondent and found that her prayer offered surprisingly little comfort. Perhaps it was because matters to do with her family were so close to her heart, she thought.

"Excuse me just a moment, Gwen." Startled, Gwen looked around to see Stuart Kirby at the kitchen door. "I just wanted to fetch another bottle for the baby."

Gwen smiled politely and nodded, and Stuart headed for the fridge. As he saw Jake busily throwing paint across his picture, he added, "You know, Peter and Adam would love to do some painting, if that's all right."

Gwen looked up at him, struck with delight at his words. "Of course, I'd love them to. I bought the paints for them really, but—what about Angela? I'm not sure she'd like them to be with me . . ." Her voice trailed off.

"She'll be busy with Rosie for the next few minutes, so I'll take the boys out of her way. She doesn't need to know I'm bringing them to you." He swept out of the kitchen, the bottle of milk in his hand, before Gwen could protest that it didn't seem entirely honest. Nevertheless, she could not ignore her pleasure at the prospect of having her grandsons join her.

Stuart's words had surprised her. She had imagined him to be of the same mind as his wife, perhaps even dominated by her to some extent, but now it seemed that he was not happy about Angela's childish rejection of her stepmother. But he had never spoken up before or in any way indicated his opinions to Gwen, who was impressed that he supported his wife in her feelings, but still asserted himself when he felt it was appropriate.

Five minutes later, Jake and Peter were firm friends and trying with little success to paint pictures of each other, while Adam waved a paintbrush in the vague direction of the paper but only succeeding in getting paint on the newspaper that covered the table, assorted kitchen appliances, and the stone floor. Gwen and Stuart laughed as they watched, Stuart sipping a mug of tea and telling Gwen about a sensitive and caring Angela whom Gwen had yet to meet. Seeing her grandsons run into the kitchen so soon after she had offered her prayer, Gwen felt ashamed and mentally chided herself for not having sufficient faith to know that her prayer would be answered in the Lord's due time.

Stuart spoke easily and unashamedly about his wife. He did not apologize for her rudeness to Gwen; he merely said that he was certain that there was a reason for her feelings, as yet undiscovered. He assured Gwen that Angela was a kind and intelligent woman, an excellent mother, and a loyal friend. Gwen had heard a similar description from Edward, but still had difficulty equating such descriptions with the discourteous and bitter woman who barely spoke to her. From the time of her marriage to Edward, Gwen had prayed daily that his children might like and accept her, that Angela's heart might be softened towards her, and that she might be accepted as Edward's new wife, and yet she still sensed such animosity from her stepdaughter that it was difficult for her to believe Stuart's claims about Angela's virtues.

She resolved to speak to Edward about it later, seek his advice, and in the meantime enjoy these rare moments with her beloved grandsons. Stuart helped her clear away the paints and clean off the stray splatters when the children were all satisfied that they had finished their pictures, and then she settled Adam on her knee and read them all a story from one of the pristine new books she had bought just for them. They might have been more comfortable in the lounge, she thought dismally as she read, but here in the kitchen there was less risk that Angela would see her with them.

<hr/>

When Bel had returned home and thanked her for looking after Jake, and Stuart had returned Peter and Adam to their mother, Gwen sought out her husband. She found him tending the garden in the sunshine and was heartened by the spontaneous kiss he gave her in greeting.

"I was just ready for a break!" he exclaimed, and she admired the neat scalloped edge he had created to the flower beds, which extended the length of the farmhouse. Edward shed his gardening gloves gladly, frowned at the mud which had somehow managed to collect under his fingernails despite them, and joined her on the wooden bench in the center of the lawn. He settled down contentedly, stretched an arm across her shoulders, and sighed in pleasure at the sight of the sparkling lake below them.

Gwen told him quickly about how pleased she was that she had been able to spend a little time with Peter and Adam, but sighed as she reflected that it had required dishonesty on Stuart's part. She had been concerned that Angela might discover them. "I pray about her every day, and yet she's just as bitter and angry as ever!" she said mournfully.

Edward hugged her comfortingly and thought for a moment before he asked, "You pray *about* her every day, don't you, my dear?" Gwen nodded in confirmation. "My dear, why don't you pray *for* her instead? Pray that she will be happy and healthy, that she will have blessings and love in her life, and that whatever difficulties and issues she has will be resolved. Don't just pray about how she relates to you. Forget yourself and just think about what is best for Angela. Will you try that?"

Gwen looked at her husband's earnest face and felt loving tears come into her eyes. Once again she had to learn a lesson about humility, and yet this time she was not hurt or discouraged. She recognized now that although Edward had been a member of the Church for such a short time, he already had astonishing wisdom and insight in matters of the Spirit. Until recently she had imagined that she still had much to teach him about the gospel, and perhaps in some respects she still did, but how much more they could learn together.

"I wonder," she said, as she stared into his kind eyes, "whether you will ever know just how much I love you."

He kissed her. "I think I do," he said.

***

After dinner the guests gathered in the lounge once again, resting as they savored the contentment of full stomachs, a warm summer's evening, and the company of friends. Angela seemed particularly tired, Gwen thought, seeing her hunched over the sleeping baby on the sofa, her eyes barely open. Whether Angela was too tired to respond with her usual scathing acrimony or whether her attitude was beginning to soften, Gwen didn't know, but when she suggested an early night for her stepdaughter, who was looking rather pale, Angela meekly agreed. She was tired, she admitted, and even bade Gwen and the other guests a polite goodnight before trudging wearily up the stairs. Gwen wondered if her prayers, now focused more on Angela's well-being, had begun to be answered already? Perhaps Angela was beginning to accept her at last.

Brian McNaught had actually enjoyed chatting with Bel over dinner. He could not remember the last time he had actually spoken with ease to someone other than his family, but Bel was quiet and gentle and listened thoughtfully and nonjudgmentally as he spoke. He had found himself telling her a little about his breakdown, about the manifold fears that plagued him each minute, and while he saw sympathy in her face, he did not equate it with the pity or scorn he so hated.

"You have been though a great deal," Bel said as they sat together in the lounge. "I've had a few difficult years myself, and it's been a challenge to keep my self-confidence and . . . hope." She bit her tongue before she added "mental health," afraid that Brian might take offense at the unintentional implication that he was in some way unstable.

"I've talked about myself too long," Brian said shyly, unaccustomed to talking at all, in particular about such personal matters. "Where are you from?"

Bel considered carefully what to say before answering and finally decided that honesty was probably the best policy. She trusted Brian after all, and he had been completely honest with her, despite his evident mortification at his loss of control over his life and emotions. She thought it ironic that after her clandestine flight to Haven and determination to maintain her secrecy and anonymity, she nevertheless seemed to be telling everyone of her situation, first Danny and now Brian.

"Actually," she said quietly, "I'm homeless at the moment, looking for a job to pay the rent, a little flat somewhere, a school for Jake."

He said nothing for a few moments and she understood that he must be taken aback by her answer. Finally he swallowed and said, as though to himself, "At least I do have that security." It was not the answer she had expected, and she doubted whether it had even been directed towards her, so she merely nodded in reply.

"Have you at least any ideas?" he asked at last.

She shrugged. "Some. Don't feel bad for me. I'm happier now, like this, than I have been for years. I've been wanting to leave for a long time."

He contemplated her without speaking for so long that she began to feel a little uncomfortable. At last he drew his wallet from his trouser pocket and pulled out a business card, studying it wistfully for a few seconds before he put it on the table in front of her. "The office phone diverts to my home number now," he said simply.

She was not sure of the significance of the card. Did he want her to phone him to let him know how she got on? Or was this an invitation of sorts? She thanked him anyway as she took the card.

"Fiona—that's my wife—would like to meet you, I'm sure. It's been a while since I could talk to someone and not feel judged, or afraid, or inadequate. I'll be needing a new secretary when I start back at work again. Can you type? I'd be happy to act as your solicitor, too. I'm guessing that you'll be needing one."

She was at once astonished and thrilled at the prospect of a job and the chance to be with someone she knew and trusted as she re-established herself and went through the trying process of divorcing Marty. Scotland was so very far away from her old life, and it was a tempting offer indeed. "I can't type, but I could learn quickly," she said eagerly. "And I will certainly be needing a lawyer. It is very kind of you, and I'll certainly consider it."

He smiled and looked away, apparently unable to say more, and Bel excused herself after a few moments. It was almost eight o'clock and she had plans for that evening.

CHAPTER 22

Bel had not taken this long to get ready for a night out since she first met Marty. She showered, washed and conditioned her hair, and then selected her best dress after trying on several and seeking Jake's disinterested opinion on each. Then she carefully applied the few items of makeup she had brought with her. When she finally stopped to look at herself in the mirror, she found herself giggling and Jake looked at her, a question in his eyes.

"I'm behaving like a teenager!" his mother laughed in answer. "It's pathetic!"

She knew that somewhere deep down in her subconscious she saw this night as something of a big date and scolded herself for imagining it. Much as she liked Steve and Danny, there could be nothing romantic in this evening. Still, in some strange way, it was a reminder to her of all that had been promised by love, and how loving and marrying the wrong person at the wrong time had shattered her young illusions. Seeing herself so carefully presented at her best, she was comforted to reflect that perhaps she had not entirely lost her belief in love, hope, and fun.

She scolded herself for imagining that there could be any romantic prospect here. She liked both the young men, Danny in particular, and was excited about spending this evening with them. But she was married—that was a simple fact—and given the jealous and grim nature of her husband, she could not bring Danny and Steve into her unpleasant little world. But just for one evening, perhaps she could join them in theirs, which seemed so much nicer than hers.

She drove her own battered old car, firing quick replies to the insults Danny heaped first on the vehicle and then on her driving ability. Then, when Steve began to add his comparisons with his own dream machine, she even threatened to leave them both at the roadside. Nevertheless, they arrived in Beddgelert without incident, to Steve and Danny's feigned surprise, stopping first at an ancient hotel and public house where a log fire blazed. True to his generous nature, Steve bought the first round of drinks, a beer for himself, Guinness for Danny, which Danny decried as inferior to the real Irish variety but drank nevertheless, and fruit juice for Bel.

Bel had wondered what they might find to talk about that evening and feared that conversation might be awkward, given that they had met only three days ago, but Danny and Steve were naturally congenial and chatted easily about their work, home life, and childhood memories. It was perhaps inevitable that their general conversation would eventually become disjointed as Bel fell into deep discussion with Danny about the latest plot twist of *Frontier,* and Steve found himself left out until he joined the loud conversation at the next table.

As Danny and Bel moved onto other topics, she had the strange sense that it was all part of a dream, that something was wrong or perhaps Danny was mocking her as, in one thing after another, they found they agreed. They had the same dislike of dried fruit, named the same dream holiday destination and perfect restaurant meal, and found their political views remarkably aligned. It was embarrassing, Bel began to feel, and pointed out that their musical taste differed, her preference being for classical. This was followed by a long discourse on the delights of Vivaldi when Danny admitted his own fondness for classical music as well as contemporary.

"Time to move on?" Steve interrupted them when his newfound friends had left.

"Sure." Danny drained his Guinness. "If my long-lost twin sister here is ready?"

They moved on to a larger pub, and Bel bought the drinks this time, allowing herself a small glass of light wine. When Danny sauntered over to the juke box, Steve began to chat to her as easily as his friend had and they were soon deep in conversation, their heads bent close together as they struggled to hear each other over the loud music.

Bel felt rather uneasy seeing Danny left out at first, until he joined the clique at the pool table and began potting some difficult shots and reveling in his own ability. Steve was pleasant, handsome, and sensitive, but he hadn't the charm and magnetism of his friend. During their conversation he repeatedly asked her about herself, encouraging her to open up and to trust him, and yet each time she evaded his questions and changed the subject.

She wondered why she should again be so hesitant to share her past when she had told Danny. Evidently Danny had kept the information to himself, respected her privacy, and she warmed yet more to him. Perhaps she had been less afraid to share her secret with Danny because they had so much in common. He was such fun and so witty and confident that she had begun to feel rather overwhelmed by him, in awe of him in a way she could never imagine she had ever been with Marty. The feelings confused her and she worried that they were inappropriate. But then, as the evening wore on and she began to glow with happiness at the alternated attentions of the young men, she realized that she could no longer ignore the fact that the warmth and wholeness she felt in Danny's presence were the first stirrings of deep affection. Given time and the right circumstances, this strange connection between them might develop into love, she thought. But under present circumstances, it was impossible.

How presumptuous to imagine that she might be at liberty to care for him, as though her feelings somehow obligated him or affected him, she scolded herself. Who was she to think that she might impose on his life in such a way, or to suppose that he might ever wish to take more notice of her than of anyone else around him? How could she ever find a place in the world he inhabited? She was nothing to him and could never hope to be more. It was wrong to even think it, wrong for Marty and wrong for Danny.

Despite the confused feelings within her, she was smart enough to know that she could not show nor state her feelings for him, but it was so difficult as they sat in that ancient public house in the beautiful and wild Welsh village not to watch him, nor to meet his gaze with one too steady as he chatted to her. She decided instead to treasure those moments, seeing him looking so fine, laughing so readily, telling sophisticated jokes that occasionally baffled Steve. These minutes would pass quickly, and she suspected that in the months and years to come she might long for this peaceful happy time with someone she felt truly understood and appreciated her.

They returned to Haven early because Bel was concerned about Jake despite the fact that he had been sleeping when they left, and Lucy was bored and starting to act up as she sat under Steve's seat. Danny had tried pouring the dog some of his drink, but she was put off by the smell.

Bel reassured herself that Jake was sleeping soundly, then joined the two young men in the lounge. There they chatted casually and waited for their adrenalized reserves of energy to wear off and sleepiness to take them. Bel was embarrassed when, in hopes of studying Danny's face as he read his book by the fire, she realized that he had closed the book and his gaze was fastened on her.

"I've just finished the latest Jacob Spillis," he said, seeing that he had her attention. "You want to borrow it?"

She brightened visibly. "How did you know I like Jacob Spillis?"

He shrugged. "Because *I* do. You like everything I like."

"Well, I'd love to borrow it if you don't mind me posting it back to you." He did not miss that point. "Is this one any good?"

"Ah!" He spread his hands in a gesture of magnitude. "What can I say? It's fantastic. You'll love it."

He held her gaze without saying anything for a while, not ashamed or embarrassed at the silence, just waiting for the appropriate moment. "Come and walk Lucy with me. Let's see if we can tire her out at last."

Steve confirmed with a knowing smile that he would listen in case

Jake awoke, and she waited at the door while Danny called the enthusiastic Labrador. Then the three of them set off, leaving the hazy glow of Haven behind them. Even though the only light came from the moon and stars, it was a fine clear night and that was sufficient.

As Lucy bounded across the hillside, Danny looked at the woman at his side and said simply, "Well, you know you can't stay here, then. It's a poor area; there were no jobs for you. You have to move on."

She nodded. She had complained to him only an hour ago that she had been disappointed to see that there were few vacancies advertised, and what little there was required a knowledge of the Welsh language or skills she did not have.

"So what *will* you be doing when you move on if you're not taking up my offer?"

She shook her head, wishing that they could just walk and be together without having to bring up the terrible things that haunted her. "I'll have to try somewhere else, somewhere bigger. I don't want to move to a city, just a small community with a good school for Jake. Then I suppose I'll contact a solicitor about my husband."

She dreaded that inevitable moment when her eyes would look upon Marty again, see him take Jake away even if it were just for a short time. Not that he was a bad father—he meant well—but he wanted to teach Jake to box, let him watch any video he wanted, even ones unsuitable for a five-year-old, and even let the boy sip beer out of his can.

Bel remembered the one time when Jake was younger she had asked Marty to baby-sit while she went to the cinema that evening with an old school friend. She had returned to find the house in darkness and neither her son nor her husband anywhere to be seen. Strangely she had not been frantic with panic that time, she had simply walked the two hundred yards to the pub on the corner and there sitting at his usual place at the bar was her husband, tiny Jake asleep in his buggy behind him, the barmaid looking nervous and wondering whether she most feared the police, the landlord, or Marty. She had been relieved when his wife had arrived to take the child home. She was used to teenagers swaggering in, trying to claim they were eighteen as they ordered their pints of bitter, but the baby was taking the underage laws to the limit, even if he wasn't drinking.

Bel knew Marty well enough even by then not to shout at him until the morning. It was a waste of energy and breath when he wouldn't remember her anger, not that he seemed to take much notice of her scolding when he was sober either. That event had effectively destroyed her social life since she never asked him to care for Jake again.

"Will your husband want access or custody?"

"I don't know. Certainly not custody—he can barely take care of himself—but he might want to see Jake once in a while. Sometimes I think it's just a macho thing; he likes telling his mates how big and strong his son is, chip off the old block, that sort of thing. He can do that just as well with a photograph. I wonder whether moving far enough away will help. If Marty has to travel too far to see Jake, then he may well not bother."

"Ireland's about as far as you can get."

"Yes." She stopped there, thinking again about going to Ireland, over the sea, another country. She had never been there either, just as she had never been to Wales before this week, and yet already both places held something special for her.

"Doesn't he love his son? Doesn't he love *you?*"

She was startled, and thrilled, to hear the astonishment in Danny's voice. It had been a long time since anyone had thought her lovable, and yet Danny's tone suggested that Marty really should love her. Of course he should; he was her husband. And perhaps in his own way, he did, in much the same way he loved beer—because of the way it made her feel and what it did for him, not because of any intrinsic worth.

"I think he does love Jake. He's proud of him anyway." Marty couldn't love Jake as she did, having missed the early crucial bonding hours. He had been on an all-nighter with Paul when her contractions had started, and it had been the friendly community midwife who took Bel to hospital and delivered the baby, just the two of them in the neat little delivery room, sharing those sweet moments with the new infant boy. Bel had left a note at the house, and Marty had turned up on the ward the next day—once he was sober enough to drive—clutching a toy rabbit he'd bought in the hospital shop, and not even knowing whether his baby was a boy or a girl twelve hours after its birth.

She stopped walking, feeling Danny's nearness, trusting him. "Thank you for everything you've done for me. You don't need to listen to all this misery. It's not your problem. You are such a good man." Her voice trailed off as she thought about how few really decent men she had met. It was cold now, she was shivering, and his eyes missed nothing. He reached out a hand to gently rub her arm for warmth, a pathetic and ineffectual movement but all he could offer until she indicated that more would be permitted.

Trembling, she gave that permission. "It's so cold."

As always he understood her, and he pulled her to him in a complete and comfortable embrace, one which imparted the warmth of both his body and his spirit and yet made her shiver all the more as she clung to him, surprised at his strength and the wonderful reality of his nearness. She let her head fall onto his shoulder, it seemed so natural that she should do so, and when she felt his head lift slightly from hers she looked up, turned towards him, and met his lips in a kiss so smooth and sensuous that she was immediately caught up in it, reveling and exulting in the soft caress of his lips, overwhelmed by a sudden rush of love and tenderness for him. He stopped briefly to look at her, smiling, then kissed her again, and then again. With each kiss, she clung to him more, wanted him more, knowing that it was wrong to kiss him but needing to do so all the same, never wanting that moment to end. They rested a while, still holding one another, foreheads pressed together, eyes lowered, not looking at each other.

"Are you happy?" he asked. It was a foolish question, he thought, knowing as he did all the fears within her, but all the same he somehow needed to know that he helped.

"Yes," she said, so he kissed her again. She could not remember Marty's kisses ever being so wonderful, even at first when she had loved him.

"Then why can't you look at me?" He was right. There was still a strange sense of guilt within her, and she could not meet his eyes, much as she wanted to. Would she find a genuine love and concern there, or would she learn from what she saw that this was just one of his childish games? Men his age did this, she knew. They used women, had lots of women. One-night stands meant nothing to them. Perhaps she meant nothing to him.

"Because this is wrong. I'm still a married woman."

He kissed her again, sweetly, lingering. "It doesn't feel wrong." His strong hands on her back didn't feel wrong either, but she forced herself to step back, twisting free of his arms. Not looking at him, she started walking again, fearing and yet still hoping for a continuation of what had started.

CHAPTER 23

S he would try not to think about it. Forget it, that was best. She called to the dog in a frail, high voice, which might also have told him it was over before it had scarcely begun. He watched her walk further up the path for a moment, then without so much as a sigh or an apology, he turned to walk back to Haven.

She did not watch him, although she saw the dog whirl round and follow him. Standing on the bitter mountainside in the moonlight, she was nevertheless aware of every step he took away from her and struggled with each one against the urge to cry his name, turn around, and run into his arms. She noticed the tears of confusion falling down her cheeks only because they left cold trails. When they had dried, she turned to walk back down the mountain to the stone farmhouse.

It was as though nothing had happened, and his usual casual demeanor was apparent when Bel reentered the lounge later and saw him chatting with Steve and teasing Lucy. He barely acknowledged her, and Steve, looking disgruntled, merely nodded. She said "goodnight," her voice faltering, and went upstairs.

Jake was sleeping still and the sight of him calmed her. She stood to watch him for a moment, hearing his steady breathing and reminding herself that real love was what she felt for her son, not this confused longing which Danny's tenderness had roused in her.

Lowering herself heavily to the bed, she pulled her knees up to her chest, hugging them in the half-light. Once again she saw her own shadowy reflection in the mirror, her eyes gleaming in the moonlight, her cheeks flushed a dramatic purple with cold and embarrassment. *He kissed me*, she murmured to her reflection, bewildered. *He kissed me. A lot.*

And are you happy about that? the dark figure in the mirror seemed to respond. She had not yet come to the point of considering whether she might be happy or sad, and she wondered where the question came from. But it was there, and there was no doubt as to her answer. She wanted to hold on to the beautiful taste of him forever; she wanted to dance and dream of him, and imagine that he had meant something by it.

But her dark other self—Lindy—chided her. *He's an immature and high-spirited boy. The feelings of those strange creatures he calls women mean little to him. And you know he'd been drinking . . .*

Bel gulped, shocked to hear Danny tarnished with the same words she had so often used when thinking about Marty. She tried to protest that he hadn't had much to drink, but realized with pathetic despair that the truth of his feelings or intentions did not matter anyway. She was married. Danny was still so young and had so much more maturing to do.

Bel let her head fall back onto the pillow and her legs flop back onto the bed. Then, without bothering to wash or change, she cried herself to sleep once more, as though her escape and the last three days had changed nothing.

***

It had been wrong, Danny knew, and in the bright reality of morning he didn't even know why he'd done it. Perhaps it had been the drink, perhaps he had simply thought she needed it, perhaps he had wanted to. She seemed so vulnerable and hurt sometimes, and she had been through so much.

But she was married, and if there was one thing he had always abhorred, it was infidelity. It had broken up his parents' marriage when he was just a child and his brother little more than a baby, and while he liked his stepfather, he could never forget seeing his mother crying and crying for days when his father had left. He and Brendan had brought her their favorite toys and teddy bears in vain.

When he grew up and found that his lively wit and courtly good looks made him a favorite with women, he had vowed never to have anything to do with the married ones, and so far he never had. It was wrong; she was someone else's wife, and whatever the state of the marriage, she was not available to him. But still . . .

Waking early, he had dressed quickly and had taken Lucy for her first walk of the day, careful not to disturb Steve. He needed the time to think, but when the walk wasn't enough, he settled in the lounge to wait out the last ten minutes before breakfast. Mrs. Anderton startled him from his thoughts only moments later, bringing him the map he had asked her for the previous evening and settling down on the sofa next to him as she opened it out to point out the route to the outdoor pursuits center. She cast a look at him as she struggled with the folds of paper and saw that his eyes, while turned towards the map, were not seeing it.

"You're very thoughtful this morning, Mr. O'Hanlon."

He smiled abstractedly. "Just something on my mind."

Remembering Edward's advice not to pry, which had proved to be so appropriate in Brian's case, she simply nodded and started explaining the route, but she could see that Danny was still not fully concentrating on what she was saying. She paused. "Perhaps we should do this later, when you've got whatever it is sorted out?"

"Mrs. Anderton," he said suddenly, "if you don't mind my asking, how long have you been married?"

She laughed, knowing that her answer would surprise him. "Three months."

He was indeed surprised. "Were you married before?"

"No, but Edward was married for a long time to a very lovely lady. They used to stay at Haven together, and then after she died, he came here alone. That's how we got to know each other."

A little embarrassed, Danny asked "Did you have . . . feelings for him when his wife was still alive?"

"Oh, no," Gwen said firmly. "I liked him. I always knew that he was a kind and generous man, but I never really thought of him in that way back then."

Danny nodded. "If you had . . . been interested in him when he was still married, what would you have done?"

She frowned, wondering. What a terrible situation that would have been. "I think I would just have had to refuse his bookings or arrange for my sister-in-law to look after Haven so that I could go away while he was here. I would have had to avoid him. I wouldn't want to do anything to encourage those sorts of feelings where they're inappropriate."

"What if his marriage had been a bad one and he didn't love his wife? What if you could have been so much better for him than she could?"

Gwen thought she could guess the reasons behind the questions, for she had seen Danny and Bel chatting happily together. With the earnest and prayerful hope that her words might be of some help as he wrestled with his dilemma, she answered patiently and honestly. "It wouldn't make any difference. Whatever state a marriage is in, it remains a marriage. Furthermore, no one outside of it can really know whether it is a happy one or not. And," she sighed, "I think too many predatory men have taken in innocent women with the claim that their wives don't understand or love them. But, of course, Edward was not like that. He did love Edith and he made that very obvious."

"So you knew his first wife," Danny said thoughtfully. "How did you feel about her?"

"I was very fond of her." Gwen's voice was steady. "We were friends and I would never have dreamed of betraying her in such a terrible way. But even if there were no love left in his marriage—or any marriage—the last thing someone needs is an illicit romance to complicate matters, and the first thing needed would be a friend."

Danny was quiet for a moment, watching her and knowing that she understood who he was talking about. "Do you think you are saying all this just because you're a religious person and believe in the sanctity of marriage?"

Gwen heard the sincerity in his voice, and again prayed for the right words. "I couldn't hope to advise you from the standpoint of my faith because you don't share it," she said forthrightly. "I might tell you what modern-day prophets have counseled on the matter, but I suspect that would mean little to you as well. I can only remind you that marriage is sacred because I know that you believe that. I've learned a great deal about you in the last few days, and I believe you are a good young man, Danny. You have standards not often seen in young people these days, but you need the strength and maturity to be able to live by them."

Danny sighed as he realized that he still would not be able to concentrate on the map.

"Do you think I might just borrow this for now and return it later?" he asked. The sympathetic smile that accompanied her nod of agreement told him that she understood.

⚜

Gwen left Danny with his map, thinking that he was a good lad with a lot to learn. Still, he seemed to have matured a great deal in just the last three days, she thought.

The lounge had filled while they were talking, and she had been so involved in speaking with him that she had not noticed her other guests leave their bedrooms and descend the stairs. The Kirby family were all scrubbed and ready, and obviously hungry. Angela was watching her closely, a frown on her face, but this time it was one of puzzlement and deep thought, not the usual scowl of hostility. Brian McNaught was standing nervously at the stairs, his hand still on the banister as though he might scamper up them back to the safety of his room at any moment, but he was smartly dressed and he smiled at Gwen as she looked up at him. She could hear the closing of another door, although she didn't know whose it was—it might have been the door to Steve's room or Bel's. Anyway, it was time for breakfast and she had chatted with Danny O'Hanlon long enough.

"Go on in, all of you, *os gwelch chi'n dda*," she called, before hurrying back into the kitchen. "Breakfast is served." She hoped that Edward had remembered to put the butter on each table.

⚜

As he sat at his table, Danny felt rather ashamed that he could not look directly at Bel. He had glanced at her briefly when she walked in, Jake's hand held tightly in hers, but he did not want to meet her eyes. As always in the mornings, she looked fair and fresh, her hair still damp from the shower and tightly tied back, a long deep-green dress complementing her eyes. Danny saw that she hardly looked up to thank Mrs. Anderton as the plate was placed before her. Perhaps she was embarrassed, too, and confused, and did not want to look at Danny either.

"I've been thinking," he said suddenly to Steve.

"Well done," his friend joked before Danny could continue. But Danny refused to be distracted.

"That little bet of ours—it seems a bit childish now. Perhaps we should just forget about it."

Steve looked surprised. "Since when did you get all responsible?"

Danny could only shrug, not knowing himself. He only knew that learning of the trials that Bel had overcome—and with such cheerfulness and competence—made his own life seem rather trivial by comparison. He felt small and foolish when he set his own experiences against hers, and now their harmless juvenile wager seemed rather unfair and inappropriate. At the hotel the two friends had often entertained themselves with similar games; the sight of a pretty young guest might inspire a bet as to which of them might snatch the first kiss or declaration of reciprocated passion.

But now Danny was thinking that it might be time they grew up, that other people could be hurt by their pranks, and that the world was not just about their own fun.

"Well, you're not getting out of it that easily just because you're losing," Steve said, his mouth full of bacon. Danny mustered his best coolly unperturbed face and raised one eyebrow at his friend, who stopped chewing and sighed noisily through his nose. "Okay, so you are winning, but a bet is a bet is a bet."

Steve kept that tone for times when he was particularly resolute, and Danny knew that he would not be persuaded to leave off. Still, whenever Danny tried to fight off the pang of pity Bel's situation inspired in him, it was simply replaced with a swelling sense of admiration for her courage and concern for her future. Being close enough to see her fine, pale skin and the darkness of her lashes against her cheek reminded him how vulnerable she had seemed last night. He could feel her thin frame as it battled against the wind, and remembered how good it had felt to enfold her in his arms.

What was wrong with him that she was getting to him like this? He had never had difficulty detaching himself from the problems of others before. Why should he care about her?

He and Steve had been so wrong to ever make that bet, to have ever thought it amusing to play with women's hearts as they had . . . but it was too late now.

CHAPTER 24

Y ou're very quiet," Stuart Kirby said to his wife as he listened
to the delicious crunching sound of rapidly melting butter
being spread on crisp toast. She was hardly eating; she hadn't
even drunk the tea, which was now going cold in its white china pot.
Rosie had been restless last night and that had awoken Adam. Perhaps
Angela was just weary. She hadn't had a really decent night's sleep
since before Rosie was born.

"I'm a little tired, that's all," Angela said, not looking at him.

"Why don't you go back to the room for a lie-down after breakfast? I'll take the kids out for a walk," he offered.

It was kind of him and she accepted gratefully. But she wouldn't
lie down, she decided. She'd sit in the lounge. It was a beautiful room
with its big inglenook fireplace, stone walls, and wonderful view
across the glacial valley.

"This is a lovely place," Stuart said, seeing his wife's half-smile as
she looked through the open doorway. He wondered what her reaction would be if he said how lucky her father was to live here and
decided not to take the risk of upsetting her.

But Angela was thinking it anyway, thinking how peaceful everything was here and how little Dad had to keep him in Birmingham.
She and Stuart and the children, of course, but they had only seen
him once a week or so anyway. Ian was busy with the company and

Netta had barely been back in Britain since she and Ian were divorced. It was sad, Angela reflected, for she and Netta had been close once, and Edward had loved his daughter-in-law.

Now that Netta had gone, Angela's weekly two-hour visit to her father's small bungalow had been little inducement to turn down a comfortable and happy life in an ancient farmhouse set on this beautiful and wild mountainside, especially one spent with a kind, loving, and honest woman by his side. She and Stuart could stay a whole week at a time here, and Dad could spend more quality time with them than he ever did during their polite but rushed visits at home, she was thinking.

She still hated that he had done it, that he had found someone and something better than them, but she could no longer deny that it *was* better. He was happy here, that was undeniable, and the path he had chosen for himself was an enviable one. She sometimes thought it would not have been so bad if her father hadn't first announced that he was joining the Mormons. To Angela, that meant people who knocked on doors, strange religious zealots who disapproved of everything. The wedding and, more recently, the family home evening had altered that perception a little, but she still wondered how her clever, sensible father had been persuaded to change his church, his life, and his habits so dramatically. Was it just love for Haven's proprietress?

After breakfast, she helped Stuart load Rosie into her baby sling and ensured that Adam and Peter were warm enough, before waving them off as they started along the mountain trail and settling into the armchair to await Gwen. She was nervous and reluctant about what she needed to say, but there were questions she needed answers to while they were still fresh in her mind, and even if they meant an unpleasant apology would be necessary, she could not put her mother's memory to rest until she had spoken to the second Mrs. Anderton about the first.

Gwen seemed nervous too, as indeed she might, to discover Angela sitting alone in the lounge, not reading, not watching television, just looking at the door waiting for her appearance. Her wariness, little masked by a smile that was barely a shadow of the one she usually wore, suggested her fear of a trap, that Angela had waited for Gwen so that she might vent her anger again. Now that she was in the room, Gwen could hardly walk away without speaking to her. She closed her eyes briefly, as though in prayer, as she sat down opposite Angela.

Angela didn't like small talk, and Gwen did not try to offer any, saying only "good morning" before allowing the younger woman to speak first.

Angela moved forward to the edge of her seat and clasped her hands, looking directly at Gwen. She drew in a sharp breath, prepared to speak, but then stopped, not knowing quite how to phrase the question.

"Did you want to say something to me, Angela?" Gwen said at last.

"Yes, I do," Angela said, but she was finding it almost impossible to formulate the words and questions she had been contemplating since breakfast. "I heard what you said to the Irish lad this morning. I wanted to know whether you meant it."

"I never say things I don't mean," Gwen answered, relieved to be spared Angela's sharp-tongued fury, at least for the moment. "What part are you referring to exactly?" She frowned a little as she tried to remember exactly what she had said.

"You—you said my mother was a lovely lady, and that Dad obviously loved her, and . . . and you said that you were very fond of her." That was the most amazing part, the part that had stunned Angela as she overheard the conversation that morning.

Gwen took a moment to answer, speaking slowly and clearly. "Yes, I loved her. I got to know her fairly well. I counted her a very dear friend."

Angela was truly amazed at the reply and shook her head as she stared at Gwen, as though seeing her for the first time. Here was an aspect of the relationship between Gwen and her parents she had never imagined. Indeed, she had almost forgotten that Gwen had ever known her mother. She tried to picture her mother as she had been during those last years, but could only remember the loud, strident voice that remained harsh, however feeble the body became, and the strong sickly smell of floral perfume she used to mask the odor of whiskey when she had been drinking. Not that her mother was a big drinker, but she did enjoy a tipple on special occasions, days which had seemed less and less special and had occurred more and more often.

Angela remembered a little more now, a face, young and certain, not frustrated and demanding as it had become in her later years. Her mother had not been a natural mother, not a loving person, but one who had instilled discipline and a sense of place in her children. Angela and Ian both had her to thank for their independence, their ambition, and their lack of fear.

"You seem surprised to hear that," Gwen said, and at her words, Angela brought herself back to the present. How could she explain, she wondered, without painting a damning picture of the woman whom it was her duty to love—as her mother herself had frequently reminded her.

"You see . . . not many people liked my mother. She was a strict parent and a hard woman. She could be demanding and outspoken, and she was never satisfied with anything. Dad was devoted to her, of course, but even I wondered whether he was relieved when she died. I know I was. He never spoke a bad word about her, ever, and when she was gone, I think we generally tried to idealize her and forget what she had been like. After all, she was our mother and we did love her."

Gwen smiled her wonderfully genuine and warm smile, and with a few words set at rest the demons which had plagued Angela for so long. "I always found her quite straightforward. She said what she meant, she knew her own mind, and she had a keen and sharp sense of humor. She was a strong personality, certainly, but not a bad person for that."

Angela found tears rising up in her eyes. "Thank you."

"For what?"

"For loving my mother. I thought nobody would now. I thought now that Dad was married again, and to somebody . . . well, *nicer* than Mother had been, he would forget her. We—Ian and I—don't really have the respect for her we should, and Stuart never met her, and the children, of course . . . I really couldn't help feeling that it was wrong to her memory that she should just be replaced like that, wiped out. It was as though I felt someone at least should be left who loved her and missed her, and that was Dad's duty. I don't want Peter, Adam, and Rosie to grow up calling you Gran as though my mother had never existed, and for all that she wasn't what she should have been, I don't think that's right."

She stopped to choke back confused tears, and Gwen reach out her hand to take Angela's, squeezing into it the much needed comfort and reassurance. Angela recoiled slightly, but tried not to show her natural resistance. She often thought it was because of her upbringing that she so disliked these emotional scenes and displays. It had made her relationship with Stuart an awkward and stilted affair at first, but over time she had begun to overcome the influence of her mother, at least within her marriage. Now she could see that this time could also be precious in laying to rest many of the issues which had most troubled her.

Looking up at Gwen, she clutched her hand gratefully. "But *you* loved her, and you remember her. You really liked her, and you were friends with her. I don't think she had many friends."

Her mother had had a great friend in Gwen, Angela realized now. Perhaps it wasn't too late for her to enjoy Gwen's friendship, too.

⁂

Gwen silently watched the tears fall, knowing the release that they brought. She felt filled with gratitude that at last she knew why Angela had seemed to dislike her so much. There was something more she could explain, she realized, that would really put the seal on Angela's understanding of the respect she and Edward held for Edith's memory. She hoped Angela would understand.

"Angela, I know you don't really know much about my faith, but there is something I should tell you about it." She paused, wondering how Angela would react to hearing about the religion she had seemed to despise. When there was no averse reaction, she continued. "As you know, next month your father and I will be flying to Salt Lake City to stay with a friend, and while we are there we will be going to God's holy temple."

"Your second wedding." Angela frowned. "Dad tried to talk to me about it, but I don't really understand what it's meant to do."

"In the temple we make special promises, which are binding not just in this life but in the life to come. Specifically we will be sealed—

this means that the marriage we already have will be made an eternal one." Gwen was so excited at the prospect she had to struggle to keep her tone level. She did not want to risk offending Angela again.

"I see."

"Edward will also be receiving his endowments. This means that your father will learn more about the gospel and make particular promises, covenants—things like obedience, honesty, faithfulness—and in return for his keeping these, he will be blessed with greater eternal opportunities in this life, and in the next, than he might otherwise have had. It is very much a life-changing event, and very special and important. The session will take place immediately before our sealing because he has to be endowed before he can be sealed to me. Now, I've already received my endowment, but I want to be there in the session with him, taking part."

Angela was listening intently and seemed to be following the difficult spiritual concepts. "So . . . what, will you make your promises again?"

"No, each person only makes them once or it would mock the whole idea. A binding covenant only needs to be made once; it is a lifetime contract. We know that these ordinances are very special and that everyone should have the opportunity to receive all the eternal blessings that might be possible, but so many people have died without even hearing about the gospel. This way we can act as proxy for them so that they can be baptized and endowed. Then, in the world to come, they have the opportunity to accept the gospel and the work done for them in the temple, and so can achieve their full eternal potential, if they so desire."

Angela nodded but said nothing, apparently intrigued.

"I will be at your father's side in that endowment session not as myself but as a representative of your mother. I will be baptized on her behalf before it begins, then I will make the promises and accept the obligations on her behalf. In that way I can extend to her the opportunity of eternal glory. It a very special act of love and service for someone who was special to Edward and me."

Angela was not a conventionally pretty woman, Gwen had often thought. She had the same clear features and strong cheekbones as Edward which, topped with her sharply cut red hair, gave her a striking and rather forbidding appearance. Gwen had reflected when she first met Angela that she would look perfect clad in dramatic tie-dyes and fringed leather; there was an unconventionality about her that clashed somehow with settled motherhood and her harmless and placid husband. Now, however, a strange radiance softened her angular features, a slow smile lit her face, and Angela was suddenly very dear to Gwen as she opened her eyes wide in wonderment, obviously touched by the thoughtful act Gwen was performing for her mother. They hugged each other briefly, spontaneously, and Gwen's belief in miracles was reaffirmed.

"What a wonderful thing—I never imagined . . . I was so wrong about you, I am sorry. I've not been myself recently, you know, with the difficult pregnancy and everything . . ."

"I understand," said Gwen, forgiving and forgetting all in the same moment that she said it. Edward was nearby, she felt. Although they had been married only three months, she could somehow sense his nearness and wondered whether he was behind the door again, listening and observing. Dear Edward would be so thrilled to see them reconciled. Perhaps she could increase his joy still further.

"Angela, my dear, I hope I'm not being presumptuous in suggesting it, but two young ladies from our church are coming to lunch tomorrow as they do every Thursday. I know they have a video about the temple. Would you like me to ask them to bring it so that you can understand exactly what it is Edward and I will be doing when we visit Salt Lake City?"

Angela looked more relaxed and at ease than Gwen had ever seen her when she agreed, with only a moment's hesitation and with the provision that this visit should not in any way be an attempt to convert or indoctrinate her. Gwen assured her that she would make this clear to the sisters, and Angela seemed satisfied with her promise.

There was just one more matter, Gwen realized, which might help reassure Angela that her mother's memory would be properly preserved. "You said the children would grow up calling me Gran. Well, Edith is actually their grandmother, and it is only proper that she should be the rightful holder of that title. I am quite happy, if you prefer, to have them call me Gwen, but I wonder whether you might allow me to be known to them as *Nain?* It's the Welsh word for grandmother, so it would mean a lot to me to hear them say it."

Again Angela agreed, with a tentative smile, which immediately turned into a yawn. There was no hiding the underlying exhaustion caused by a long and difficult pregnancy coming so soon upon the last, and weeks of nights broken by the shrill cry of a nevertheless beloved baby. From his place just outside the open doorway, Edward watched with satisfied pleasure as Gwen suggested that she care for the children that morning while Angela went back to bed and slept, and delight when Angela readily agreed that it would be good for Peter, Adam, and Rosie to spend some quality time with their Nain.

CHAPTER 25

B el tried to forget her confusion as she cajoled her son into brushing his teeth, washing his egg-smeared face, and then making his bed, but Danny's tender voice and words kept ringing through her mind. She found herself looking wistfully through the window, trying to locate in the shimmering daylight the exact place where his kisses had melted away her fear last night. She wished she had someone to talk it through with. As if she hadn't enough problems, Danny was a distraction she could ill afford.

She had decided to turn her job-hunting efforts to Bangor that day. The cheap local guidebook she had picked up indicated that it was the nearest city, although with only twenty thousand inhabitants, it barely warranted the title. There was a university there, where work might be found, and a hospital, and it was nestled amidst the mountains in this tranquil land, and therefore safe. She thought with satisfaction of that safety and found herself imagining Danny's arms around her again. She would be unable to concentrate, she realized, unless she dealt with her tangled feelings first. She had to speak to Amy.

They had not been close as children, but adulthood brought new understanding and Bel had confided in Amy about every trouble and disappointment over the last few years and always received new strength and courage from her. Mrs. Anderton again waved away her offer to pay for the call, and thoughtfully invited Jake through to the kitchen where Adam and Peter were busy stamping out potato prints. Grateful for the solitude, Bel dialed the number and the sound of Amy's cheerful voice was enough to lift her spirits. Quickly, and with more than a little embarrassment, Bel explained the situation to her sister.

"I think it's great," Amy said, and Bel could almost hear her jumping for joy at the news that someone apparently cared about her sister. "Go for it. You deserve a decent man after so long with that thug you married."

Bel shook her head in despair. "Go for what? In a couple of days, we'll all go our separate ways and I'll never see him again, and in the meantime I'm married to Marty. Besides which, I don't know what he meant by kissing me, perhaps he was just trying to cheer me up, or saying goodnight, perhaps he'd had too much to drink—"

"Well, how much had he had?"

In a voice which was even more subdued than before, she said, "Two pints."

"Two pints! Marty and Paul used to drink at least seven and still think they were having an articulate conversation. Look, what does it matter? He sounds like a nice guy, have some fun while you can."

Bel sighed heavily. "It matters because six years ago I promised in front of all my family and friends—including you, I might add—to love, honor, and respect Martin Hunt and to be faithful to him until I die. I know he's broken his vows often enough, but that doesn't mean I should."

"I see—so you still love, honor, and respect him, do you?"

This was getting her nowhere, Bel thought in frustration. Amy just did not seem to understand just how complicated the situation was. She did not view marriage with the same awe that her sister did. As a child, Bel had dreamed of the day she would float up the aisle in a beautiful sweeping white dress, and she had envisaged happy years with her prince charming and well-behaved fresh-faced children. Marty's romantic proposal had been all she had hoped for, the marriage itself less so, but the ideal still lived. It was no good talking to Amy. She was still young and naive, and understood little about the obligations of matrimony. None of her many boyfriends had lasted beyond a few months, and mopping up the tears inherent in her sister's disastrous union had convinced Amy that the foolishness which accompanied blind love was best avoided.

Bel asked briefly whether Amy had heard anything from Marty and was heartened to learn that Amy had not seen or heard from him since she had told him that his wife was safe and well and filing for divorce. Bel thanked Amy for her help, and replaced the receiver, pleased that Marty seemed to have taken the news so well but reasoning sadly that if she wanted comfort and good advice, she needed to speak to someone who understood the sacred nature of marriage. Danny, she realized, was probably one such person. He shared so many of her opinions and preferences, she imagined he, too, would value marriage despite his actions and words the previous night, but she could not speak to him. She was too ashamed and afraid.

When the opportunity presented itself, she decided, she would speak to Mrs. Anderton. But not today. Today she would try to forget anything had happened between Danny and herself as she headed for Bangor, focusing her mind on finding a job and building a new future.

<hr />

Even from the outside, Amy Crosby's flat was as fussy and fastidious as the woman herself, with lacy festoon net curtains showing in the sparkling windows behind heavy, lined, embroidered drapes adorned with neatly set valances and tie-backs, and cheap china ornaments arrayed across the sills. Marty forced a smile onto his face as he and Paul climbed the single flight of stairs to the door that read "Lakeview" below the number. What sort of pathetic woman would name a flat, he wondered, especially when the only view it afforded was of the oil refinery.

Amy was the opposite of her sister—shamelessly overweight and stereotypically cheerful, at least until the moment she saw who it was at her door. Fat women shouldn't wear tight jeans, Marty wanted to tell her, but instead he bit his tongue and asked whether he and his brother might come in to talk about Lindy.

"I don't know where she is," Amy said stubbornly.

"I just want you to pass on a message to her," Marty said, trying to sound reasonable. "Can we come in and discuss it?"

After a moment's thought, Amy stood aside and the brothers squeezed past her. She led them into the over-decorated living room but did not invite them to sit down, just stood, arms folded, waiting for Marty impart his message. Marty realized at that point that he had not thought of a suitably convincing message and was pleased when his brother, presumably sensing that their time here might be limited, apologetically asked whether he might be directed to the bathroom. Amy waved him off down the corridor without a thought.

"So what's this message then?"

What indeed? Marty's mind raced. "Just tell her I want her to come home."

His sister-in-law snorted. "I'll bet you do. Want some real home cooking again, I suppose? Or have you run out of clean clothes?"

Under any other circumstances he wouldn't stand to let her talk to him like that, but he let it pass, just curling up his fists behind his back and digging his nails into his palms as he fought his anger. "Tell her I miss her. Tell her if she comes home, I won't hold this against her. We'll just forget about it and pretend it never happened. I can understand that she might not be thinking straight." He remembered something else and tried to sound tender and caring. "She's been a bit ill recently, hasn't she? She's not really herself, probably not quite in her right mind. I'll put this down to that and forgive her totally."

Amy stared at him, seeming incredulous. "Oh yes, well, obviously. A bit ill. You're referring to the week she spent in hospital with appendicitis, I presume? I think I can safely say that thanks to that week away from you, she is thinking straighter than she ever has before. I'll give her your message, but I will certainly not be advising her to come back to you. But thank you so much for your gracious munificence in offering to forgive her."

Amy's voice was sharp with sarcasm and Marty began to feel a little uncomfortable as well as angry. Luckily at that moment Paul breezed in, nodding at his brother to confirm that the task was accomplished, and that there was no reason for them to stay. They left so quickly that Marty worried for a moment that Amy might be suspicious that his message had not been the real reason for their visit, but he no longer cared anyway. They were a step closer.

They returned to Marty's empty home, and he fetched the beers from the fridge while Paul flopped onto the sofa. It was surprising, Marty thought, returning with the cold cans, how shabby the room looked after such a short time of neglect. The carpet was encrusted with evidence of his take-away lifestyle—batter from the fish, dried-out bean sprouts, and grains of rice nestled deep into the wool pile. There was a thick layer of dust over every surface, and newspapers and empty beer cans lay across the floor. Marty mentally assured himself that it looked worse than it was because of the contrast with Amy's immaculate and elaborate apartment.

Five numbers were scrawled on Paul's pocket notebook, hastily copied from the little caller display unit Amy had next to the telephone in her kitchen. Marty recognized one as belonging to Lindy and Amy's mother. Two of the numbers had local codes, and he doubted he would find his wife at either of those, since he expected that she had tried to go as far away as possible. So it had to be one of the other two.

"This one was on there twice," Paul said, jabbing a finger at the final number. Marty nodded, but he liked to work in strict order. Nervously he dialed the first of the two numbers which had unfamiliar codes. The telephone was answered almost immediately by a cheery young woman who sang out, "Clearsky Windows, Victoria speaking. How can I help you?"

Marty felt a little guilty at hanging up so soon when the girl had obviously hoped for a commission-earning order, but he smiled to himself all the same. He was one step closer to locating his wife. That last number had to be hers.

CHAPTER 26

Brian McNaught had come to trust and depend on his counselor over the last few months, but as he sat in the deep sill of the small window in his room at Haven, he wondered if Elaine might have been wrong about this break. She had felt that some time on his own would be good for him, but he realized that instead of overcoming his fear of the world beyond his home, he had begun to feel that this ancient farmhouse with its thick granite walls was a refuge from all the pains of the world. His troubles were still out there, but he was safe here.

Seeing the summer breeze ruffling the grass outside, he pressed his hand to the leaded window pane and was comforted to feel only stillness. Even the elements were kept at bay here, and all his terrors were far away. He felt a shudder run through him at the memory of his office, the town, the faces of angry clients, and he felt the black fear and despair welling up again like bile into his heart. He pressed his eyes tightly shut, and when he opened them again, he saw that he was still safe, here in his stone fortress on a Welsh mountainside.

Elaine had recommended that he take some time to himself to rest, to develop his confidence and relax through his painting, and to give Fiona some time alone without the stress of caring for him. After numerous twice-weekly counseling sessions, he felt confident enough to make the journey, and Elaine had helped him choose Haven as the ideal location for him to recuperate. She had been right. It was peaceful and beautiful and perfect, but now he wondered if he might be afraid to leave and return home, back to everything which had sent him here in the first place.

For every hour he had spent painting, he thought, he had spent another hour just sitting here in his room, staring down at the rugged landscape and yet not really seeing it. In its place he had contemplated the darkness that surrounded him and the narrow shaft of light that was slowly banishing it. Elaine had taught him to visualize warmth and light and comfort, and as he sat close to this window he imagined the warm rays enveloping him and filling this cheery room, lighting every dim corner with hope and promise.

He had developed a great fear of people in the later stages of his illness, when client after client seemed to be angry and accusatory, or demanding and relentless, until he had finally sent his secretary home, locked the door, and unplugged the telephones. He still feared people a little, even those he had never met, conscious of their potential to hurt him. They could be so unpredictable, so difficult to understand. Just as he thought he might fathom their motives or personality, someone he cared about would do something completely out of character and unexpected, and he would realize again how much he was at the mercy of the whims of others. Lately their pity had been worst of all, and when Fiona had encouraged all those around him to behave normally, they had overcompensated and become painfully false.

Animals, land, the sun, those he understood. Every day they were the same. Every morning here, he would see the mountains standing as bleakly proud and firm as they had always stood, and the same sun would light them, casting the same beautiful shadows and highlighting the same rocky crags he had painted yesterday. Each day he could set up his easel and know that he would face the same landscape, identical sheep still grazing the fields, the bright lake still reflecting the warm sun. It was reassuring to encounter such stability in this confusing, uncertain world.

People were more complicated. He was less fearful of them now, but he continued to find it difficult to talk to others and knew he often seemed curt and abrupt, even offensive. He thought he had managed to overcome this a little, as he had grown to trust those around him. He even felt something akin to warmth when he remembered Gwen Anderton's encouraging smile or Bel Hunt's honesty and vulnerability. In only two days he would leave this safe place and he felt some trepidation at the thought, but he thought, too, that he had found some peace and strength. Perhaps that would be enough to go on for now.

Below his window, Brian saw little Peter Kirby run into view pursued by his brother, the wobbly toddler, Adam. He heard Gwen's laughter somewhere further off, and he smiled to himself. Coming to Haven had reminded him what happiness was, and that he had known it once before. It would be good to see Fiona and the children again, he thought.

⁂

Edward Anderton was in remarkably good health for his age and more than capable with keeping up with the lively games of his grandchildren as they chased balls and rode imaginary horses around the gardens which surrounded Haven. He was less used to the summer sun, however, and as the thermometer indicated that the temperature was climbing towards the eighties, he left the children in the care of his delighted wife and returned to the coolness of the stone house, settling into his favorite armchair with a book and more than a little contentment.

The harsh double ring of the phone broke the spell cast by the detective novel, and he sighed as he left the comfort of his seat to answer it. "Good afternoon, Haven Guest House. Can I help you?" It was Gwen's preferred method of answering the phone; she so liked to give a good impression to potential guests. On this occasion, however, there was nothing but silence from the receiver. He tried again. "This is Haven. Can I help you?"

A gruff yet nervous voice asked, "Haven?"

"Yes," Edward said patiently.

"A guest house?"

"Yes. Do you think you might have the wrong number?"

The man answered quickly, "No, no. Actually I was looking for a guest house. Whereabouts are you?"

"About halfway between Llanberis and Beddgelert."

There was another long pause before the voice hesitantly asked, "And where would that be?"

Edward marveled at the ignorance of someone who could manage to choose a guest house without knowing exactly where he wanted to stay. With something like incredulity, he said, "Snowdonia, North Wales," and resisted the urge to add a sarcastic comment along the lines of "You know, left a bit from England, on planet Earth." Instead he asked whether the caller would like him to send a brochure, but was answered only with a click and hum as the mysterious man hung up.

Edward replaced the receiver, looked at the phone in confusion for a moment, then shrugged and returned to his comfortable chair and his novel. If whoever it was decided he wanted to book a room after all, he'd call back. There was no point wasting time worrying that he might have lost a booking.

CHAPTER 27

As she awoke on Thursday morning, Bel found her spirits at a low ebb. In spite of her hopes, Bangor had offered little suitable employment, most of the advertised vacancies demanding at least a working knowledge of the Welsh language. She felt safe and at home here in the rural beauty of Wales, but much as she wanted to settle here it seemed impossible. Time was running out, she did not want Jake to start school later than the other children, and yet the new school year began in less than three weeks and they still had nowhere to live.

For the first time, she began to feel that she had too much to cope with. After years of planning, she had finally escaped, left Marty to find her own way in the world, and yet there seemed to be no suitable employment anywhere. Added to that was the uncertainty of her confused feelings for Danny. She was entirely alone and shouldering a burden so large that she doubted her slight, thin frame could carry it any longer. Perhaps the time had come to swallow her pride and ask for help.

Bel sought out Gwen soon after breakfast and found her in the dining room clearing the tables. She had the strangest feeling that Gwen had been half expecting her from the way the older woman smiled, put down her tray, and pulled out two of the dining room chairs for them to sit on.

"Mrs. Anderton, I . . . I need some advice. I thought perhaps you could help."

Gwen sat down and nodded to indicate that she would happily give whatever advice she could. Despite the older woman's patient and accepting face, Bel found it hard to know where to begin and decided to offer the easier problem first. "I'm trying to find a job and settle down somewhere, get Jake into school. I had hoped it might be in this area, it is so lovely here, but I've been to the job centers at Porthmadog and Pwllheli on Tuesday, then Bangor and Caernarfon yesterday, and there just doesn't seem to be much work available."

Gwen thought for a moment before replying. "There isn't much in this area except the tourist trade, which is seasonal, of course. You might have a little more luck heading back along the coast towards Rhyl and Wrexham. There's quite a bit of industry up there, and the Welsh language isn't used as much as it is here. I believe there are plenty of jobs and cheap housing, but the communities are still fairly small and friendly. It takes less than two hours to get to Rhyl from here, so you should have plenty of time to look for opportunities there if you leave fairly soon."

Bel was relieved to hear that there was hope that she might find employment, and was just wondering whether she might go on to confide her entire situation to Gwen when the older woman gently asked, "If you don't mind my prying, I sense there is a bigger problem. I'm here to help if I can."

She was a good person, Bel knew, honest and caring, and she had already helped so much just by directing her to towns where she might be more likely to find work. It had felt so good finally to tell Brian and then Danny the truth yesterday, even if it had led to a confusing turn of events. Undoubtedly Gwen would be able to offer yet more support and comfort.

"I . . . er, I've just left my husband. He wasn't a very nice character. I was miserable and I needed to get away. This is the first place I've come to."

Gwen smiled again, encouragingly. "Would you like to talk about it? Was he very unkind?"

"No, I wouldn't like to talk about it. It was very unpleasant, but it's over, and now I'm finally beginning to feel quite hopeful and happy. I never thought I would; it's quite surprised me. Perhaps it's this place; it's so peaceful and everything feels so good here. There's a marvelous atmosphere. Or perhaps it's . . . well, I've started to see that not all men are as bad and that I still have my life and opportunities ahead of me. I can really live again, and I can make my own decisions and go through whole days without having anything to fear. I can . . . well, it's hard to explain."

Gwen's tone was quiet and nonjudgmental as she asked, "Is Danny O'Hanlon complicating matters for you, my dear?"

Bel looked at Gwen with wide blue eyes, but she had known how observant Gwen was. Seeing Bel and Danny together, she had obviously guessed at their growing friendship.

"He's everything I hoped Marty would be, and isn't. He's bright, witty, fun. He respects me and listens to me and laughs at my jokes. He's sympathetic when I'm sad. We have everything in common, and I really think we're on the same wavelength; we understand each other in such a strange way sometimes. Since I am planning to divorce Marty as quickly as possible, would it be so wrong if I were to let Danny know how I feel about him now?"

Gwen didn't hesitate. "Yes, it would," she said gently, "and you know it would. You're still married, Bel, and you have barely discovered your own freedom and self-confidence. You have so much ahead of you and so many difficult times to face, and I think there is a real danger that you will just transfer all your hopes to Danny and lean on him to help you through it. And much as I like Danny, I really don't think he needs that. I'm not sure he's mature enough or strong enough, and it would be a very bad idea to bring him into your situation at this stage."

She was right, Bel acknowledged, as she sadly concluded that she had met Danny at the wrong time. And now, in just a few days they would part, and she would never see him again. He would return to his life in Ireland, meet someone else, perhaps marry and have a family, and they would never have taken that chance to see whether something more between them might have happened.

She was angry at herself again for being foolish enough to marry so hastily. She had been angry at herself for years now, but here again she seemed to be paying for that mistake, as if she had not paid enough in enduring five years of a cruel and torturous marriage. And yet, without the impetus of a harsh husband to escape from, she would never have come here and would never have met Danny at all, never even have had the small pleasures that knowing him had brought. Amidst the self-blame, for the first time she felt some good might have come from her unbearable situation.

She had not really needed the older woman's advice about Danny; she had known all along what was right. She had merely needed encouragement to find the strength to do it. She left Gwen Anderton with her thanks, assuring her that she would do as Gwen advised, although Bel wished she could demonstrate more conviction in her voice, and see greater satisfaction in the older woman's face.

⁎

Gwen found herself wringing her hands like some eccentric old character in a melodrama as she watched the young woman leave the dining room, head down but with a firm step, as though ascending the gallows to her own execution. Gwen might have laughed at herself for creating such an extreme picture, but it had already been an emotionally taxing few days, and she was too wrung out to see anything amusing in her thoughts.

From their first meeting, there had been something in Bel's stalwart yet fragile appearance which had told Gwen something was wrong. Now she knew in part what Bel had suffered, and felt not only a profound pity but extreme anger toward anyone who would treat such an innocent so badly that she would take her child and flee to a strange place with only a battered old car and a suitcase full of clothes to call her own.

She had wondered what the cause for Bel's early morning arrival and apparent nervousness might be and, even not knowing, had sympathized with her plight. She understood that some men could be cruel and often did not show their true colors until after marriage. Courtships could be so quick these days and might be conducted so superficially that it was not surprising when marriage ended up not a partnership of equals but one of victor and victim.

In some small measure, Gwen thought she knew how wonderful it must now feel for Bel to be free again. Gwen had lived alone for a long time before she had married, and her marriage appeared to be everything that Bel's had not been. There was no hint of fear or oppression in Gwen's own marriage, of course, although choices still had to be considered jointly. Seeing that Edward had his own expectations, traditions, and ways of doing things, she had had to adapt and compromise to them. It was not easy, but neither was it unpleasant, and she was already growing used to some of the little differences. Edward had also had to give up many of the things he liked—a long lie-in with the morning paper, whole milk, and watching football in bed late at night—but being together more than compensated for the inevitable changes.

Bel was a woman who had given up far more, who through her marriage had lost the right to live with self-respect and without fear, who had been daily used, taken for granted, and dictated to, insulted and ignored until she had taken her beloved child and left, late at night, without a word. It was little wonder she felt such a blessed release. And even less a wonder, perhaps, that she had been overwhelmed at the attentions shown to her by Danny O'Hanlon.

Gwen had advised Bel to do what she knew was right, but still she wavered over whether it was best for the younger woman. But how could Gwen doubt it? She knew how sacred marriage was; how was it that she was already wishing she had told Bel to forget Marty and speak to Danny immediately? Gwen sighed, wondering at her contradictory emotions, and thinking perhaps she was merely tired, after caring for three small children yesterday and a lively five-year-old the day before that.

Edward had come up silently behind her, and she jumped slightly when he put his hands on her shoulders. He had an uncanny knack of knowing when she needed him and she turned and hugged him close, tears filling her eyes. "What's wrong?" he asked, a tender look in his eyes.

"Wickedness never was happiness," she murmured, mostly to herself, like a mantra. "Choose the right."

"*What?*" Edward asked, baffled. "Is something wrong, my dear?"

"I just advised someone to do the right thing, but I'm not sure myself if that's what she ought to do. Bel Hunt, the poor lamb—she's been hurt so much already, and I've just advised her to do something that may well destroy the best chance of happiness she's had for a while and perhaps cause her even greater pain."

Edward put a comforting arm around her shoulders. "I came to tell you that the missionaries have arrived, my dear. They're in the lounge with Angela and Stuart and the children. Are you feeling up to coming to join us? Don't worry about the clearing up in here. You know the sisters love to help with that. I suspect that's why they're here so early—unless they're hungry, of course!"

Gwen hesitated. "That's a happy thing, isn't it? Angela and Stuart speaking to the missionaries? It should cheer me up."

She was trying to talk herself into a mood she did not truly feel, and Edward could hardly fail to notice. "Are you having doubts? About what is best for Bel and whether you advised her to do the right thing? Because we don't know the grand scheme of things, Gwen. We only know what is right and wrong according to what is set out in the scriptures and told us by the prophets, and it is not always easy to do what is right, but ultimately it is always for the best. You have such a strong faith; you have to have faith that if Bel does what is right, it will eventually bless her life and you will be blessed for helping her."

He had always been so wise in everyday matters, and now he had a new spiritual wisdom that still surprised and delighted Gwen, no matter how many times she had observed it over the last few months and days. She was proud of her Edward, and now it was time to put Bel Hunt out of her mind. Sister Morrison and Sister Keene were in the lounge, smiling and talking with her new stepdaughter and son-in-law and grandchildren. She had not dared hope for this moment, and she wanted to enjoy it to its fullest. She kissed Edward and followed him into the lounge, but kept a prayer in her heart for Bel Hunt.

CHAPTER 28

Angela had grown used to the pounding headaches which had plagued her for the last few months, but as she joined Stewart in meeting the missionaries from her father's church, she found it difficult to ignore the pain that crept insidiously across her temples and sent ripples of pain between her ears. Her doctor had told her that her frequent headaches were caused by stress, and she had easily seen how her daily grind and lack of sleep might lead to physical symptoms. But, she argued with herself, she was now feeling more rested and content than she had for many years. So why the headache now?

The day before, she had slept deeply and blissfully while Gwen cared for her children, and then had awakened slowly, deliciously warm and contented, feeling a renewed sense of her worth and individuality. She was not just a mother today; she was Angela again.

Wanting to cherish each private moment, she had lain in bed for almost an hour, awake but not moving, just thinking about her father, her mother, her children. She found to her astonishment that she missed Peter, Adam, and Rosie. She had seen them only a few hours ago, and she knew they were not far away, but temporarily freed from the burden of cajoling them, waiting out their tantrums, mopping up their tears and worse, she found that she loved them. They were not just a burden on her, not just work and exhaustion, but her bright and beloved children.

And her mother. Had Edith loved her as she loved Peter, Adam, and Rosie? The evidence was not obvious, but her own children might now be hard pressed to see evidence of affection in her, strained and harassed as she always was. She resolved to endeavor in the future to leave her own offspring in no doubt of her devotion to them.

She was ashamed that she had been so wrong about Gwen. The circumstances under which they had met had obscured the reality of Gwen's character. Angela formed her opinion of Gwen the day Edward announced that he was dating again and planned to convert to his new love's religion. Having to relinquish her position as the primary object of her father's attention had hurt her more than she liked to admit, and her guilt, as she remembered her mother, had crystallized her hatred of the unknown woman who had usurped Edith's place.

His new religion, which had at first seemed to be some strange way in which her father might be shaped and subdued, now seemed to be a joyous and worthy faith, which Edward had entered willingly and with full understanding of what it encompassed and entailed. Angela saw, too, that her father's new wife was a kind and thoughtful woman, honest and warm, self-sacrificing and generous. It was not surprising that her father had fallen in love with Gwen, nor with this beautiful old farmhouse where he had chosen to live the rest of his life.

While still lying in bed, Angela found by raising her head slightly, she could see the stunning view across the sunny valley. She thought how uplifting it must feel to awaken every morning to that sight and to the nearness of someone so beloved. She was feeling happier and more optimistic than she had for many months, now that she had found some resolution to the worries which had troubled her since her father's marriage. With that acknowledgment, she had returned to find her children playing happily with their grandmother and, watching them, had felt the final resolution fall into place.

No longer tired or stressed, Angela had looked forward to the video that the two cheerful young women promised would explain the purpose and significance of her father and Gwen's second wedding. So why was her headache still troubling her, Angela wondered. Seeing her pale complexion and pained eyes as she sat beside him, Stuart put a comforting hand over hers. With the other, he fumbled in his shirt pocket and brought out a packet of paracetamol tablets, which she accepted with gratitude.

Angela watched Gwen as much as she did the video over the next half hour. Her hostess's habitual warm smile had been replaced by an expression of serene solemnity and her bright eyes darted across the screen almost hungrily, taking in every detail of the exquisitely beautiful buildings and interiors depicted there. It confused Angela a little, for she already knew that Gwen had already visited these temples and must be familiar with them, and yet she watched with an air of innocent wonder, her lips sometimes mouthing the words of a gentle background hymn. As the video ended, Angela concluded that Gwen had a profound love for these special places, and a reverence for whatever life-shaping ceremonies she had participated in there.

Sister Morrison switched off the television and turned, smiling, to Angela and Stuart. Adam was sitting peacefully on her lap, Angela noticed for the first time, and was surprised. He did not often take to strangers. "Sister Anderton already told us you didn't want to hear a lesson," Sister Morrison said. "But I sense you might like us to answer some questions for you."

Angela had settled comfortably into the sofa and was feeling tranquil and drowsy, and thought for a moment she would have preferred just to relax further and just listen to the melodic accents of the young women as they spoke. Asking questions seemed to be a task that required more energy and attention than she, in her sleepily contented state, felt able to give. She was pleased to hear Stuart immediately accept the suggestion and begin putting to the missionaries the queries they had both had for the last year. She wondered whether her sensitive husband realized she just wanted to listen.

Why was it necessary for Edward to be baptized again? Why had he stopped drinking tea, coffee, and alcohol? Why had the sisters themselves come as missionaries to an already Christian country? Their many questions were answered with clarity and patience, and Angela found her initial fears about this strange new religion fading into respect for the devotion and genuine faith that the sisters and Gwen shared.

Stuart seemed satisfied with the answers he received, and Angela roused herself to ask a final question. "Why are they having to fly all the way to America for this second wedding?"

Sister Keene looked thoughtful. "There is a temple just a few hours from here, so . . . I guess you'd have to ask them that." She smiled towards Gwen, but it was Edward who replied.

"I wanted to go there, to see the Salt Lake Temple, and make this special day even more memorable. It's . . . I don't know, I suppose it's like a pilgrimage for me. There's something truly wonderful about that particular temple, where faithful Saints have been making sacred covenants for over a hundred years. Plus it gives Gwen a chance to catch up with some friends, do some shopping—and it'll be our honeymoon, too. And I wanted Gwen to have a proper wedding dress."

At this, Gwen looked at her husband in surprise. "A proper dress?"

He blushed a little. "That suit you wore for our wedding was very nice and you did look beautiful, but it wasn't really a proper wedding dress, was it?"

She laughed. "I couldn't wear a frothy, flouncy thing at my age!"

He leaned closer. "But for the sealing you'll have to! I know that temple dresses have to be white, and they have to be floor length, and you can get a really nice dress and a veil and really look like a bride. You shouldn't be denied that chance to look really special for your wedding just because you married late in life, and in Salt Lake there'll be so many lovely dresses to choose from. I wanted to take you shopping for a really wonderful wedding dress."

Gwen was touched beyond words. She had felt a little wistful on her wedding day three months ago as she looked into the mirror and saw herself in the knee length white linen suit she had decided was more appropriate. Edward understood her better than she had realized. "I already have a temple dress, my love." She smiled. "But I don't think I'll be packing it."

It was a touching moment and Angela felt almost that they were intruding, but she forced her mind back to the issues which had most occupied her recently. She had imagined up until now that her father had been led into this church by Gwen, had joined it for her, and continued to attend regularly and do all that was required of him because of his obligation to his wife. Now she realized that Edward held a conviction that was in every way as strong and deeply held as Gwen's. It raised yet more questions, and she forgot her tiredness as her curiosity led her to question further.

"Dad . . . do you truly believe this religion to be true?"

Edward's answer was quick and determined. "I know it."

"I—I had thought that you just converted so that you could marry Gwen."

Gwen answered quickly. "I would not have let him. If I had thought for a moment that he did not really have a testimony of the gospel of Jesus Christ, I would not have married him. And I doubt that the missionaries would have allowed him to be baptized if they had imagined that he did not truly feel the Spirit guiding him."

Angela nodded slowly, letting this new knowledge further change her perception of her new stepmother from the domineering querulous woman she had imagined to the honest, warm, loving, and devout woman now before her. She wondered whether she had not imagined Gwen to be a clone of her own mother? Perhaps somewhere she had believed that her father had chosen for himself another demanding, discourteous wife, one who had first insisted that he leave behind the doctrines of his upbringing to convert to her preferred philosophy, just as he had to leave his home and family to live in her isolated and bleak home. The reality was that Gwen could not be more different from Edith, and Angela found herself even more touched that Gwen had loved her mother so dearly.

Seeing the sister missionaries reminded her that she had been in the process of establishing the depth of her father's faith. "If you had split up, Dad, if it hadn't worked out and you two hadn't got married . . ." Angela paused, feeling awkward.

"I would have stayed in Birmingham and attended the LDS church there."

Angela nodded, understanding at last, and even more ashamed that she had jumped so easily to conclusions which bore no relation to the truth. She felt satisfied, completely at ease, at last, that her father was happy, that he had done what was right, and that she need no longer be concerned for him. She realized, too, at that moment, that her headache had completely gone.

Sister Morrison asked whether they might like to learn a little more about the church, and Stuart accepted for them both, seeing that his wife no longer felt suspicious or bitter towards this religion, and knowing that she loved to learn. First, though, Edward reminded them, there was a delicious light lunch awaiting them in the dining room.

CHAPTER 29

J ake pushed the vegetable around the plate with an expression of horror contorting his face that grew deeper each time his mother patiently insisted he eat his broccoli. Bel gave up more quickly than usual, trying to reassure herself that his growth was unlikely to be stunted for life because of three uneaten broccoli florets. Instead, she redirected her efforts at persuasion inwardly to herself.

Today had been a good day, she told herself firmly. She had been able to unburden herself to Gwen, who had been very helpful and sympathetic. She had found many employment opportunities in Wrexham, two of which seemed particularly promising and offered walk-in interviewing, and had even found a well-priced basement flat to rent in a nearby village close to a small primary school. On the way back, they had stopped in Beddgelert for some delicious ice cream in a variety of flavors, such as crème caramel, which she had never imagined might exist, and now they had a delicious dinner—their last at Haven—to enjoy. So why was she so despondent when this day seemed to have brought her so much hope?

The answer was sitting only a few feet away from her, she realized, energetically shaking huge and unnecessary dollops of tomato ketchup over his braised pork chop. She was still confused over her feelings for Danny, and in particular on the meaning and significance of the tender moments they had shared on the mountainside. He had barely said a word to her in the days since then, neither to apologize for his inappropriate behavior if it was not intended to convey attraction, nor to affirm his affection for her. She was left uncertain and uneasy, and knew that however easily matters might fall into place with regard to her future, she needed to resolve the situation with Danny before she could happily settle into any new life.

He seemed to be avoiding her gaze, watching Steve intently as they spoke, or when they were silent, focusing on his plate, and even looking down at the pleading-eyed dog under his chair when he finished his food. It was not natural for him, she knew. He was usually alert and gregarious, and his eyes would dart over the entire room, taking in all the detail and information they could. On other days he had exchanged jokes with fellow guests, but he did not today. Bel wondered whether he sensed her eyes on him, for he seemed to hurry through his dessert and was the first to leave the dining room without even a glance in her direction.

Bel tried to ignore his apparent indifference so she could enjoy every spoonful of Gwen's steaming rice pudding with a generous dollop of strawberry jam in the middle. Jake grew restless as soon as he had eaten his dessert, and Bel let him go through to the living room without her, being in no hurry to confront Danny with her desire to discuss her confusion. She lingered over her coffee, enjoying her talk with Brian McNaught, whom she had invited to sit at her table that evening. Although not the most forthcoming conversationalist and certainly not possessed of the lightning wit Danny had, Brian was a pleasant and thoughtful man.

At last they wandered slowly into the lounge where she saw that Jake was tickling the dog in the far corner close to Danny and Steve, and was pleased to have an excuse to join them. Danny did not acknowledge either her approach nor her presence, and now she was certain that he had been hoping to avoid her, perhaps even to leave the next day without speaking to her. She could not let that happen. But at least Steve smiled at her, so she addressed her question to him. "What time are you two leaving tomorrow?"

"Soon after breakfast. Our ferry leaves at noon," he replied.

"I'd better go and pack," Danny said, standing up hastily, and stepping over the recumbent dog as he almost ran to the stairs. She could not let him do it; she needed to speak to him. She followed him and quietly called his name as he reached the foot of the stairs. He paused for a moment but did not respond. As he reached out for the handrail, she spoke louder, more urgently, "Danny—I need to speak to you." Seeing that everyone had heard, she cringed inwardly in embarrassment.

"In a while, then. I'm busy at the moment," he said quietly, still not looking at her.

"No, now," she said, knowing that with the others watching, he could not object. He said nothing but went to the front door and she followed him. Strangely enough, as soon as the door closed behind them, he seemed to relax, and even managed to look at her and smile. They walked in silence a little way along the mountain path, and as the ground underfoot became steeper and a little rocky he took her hand, intertwining his fingers with hers.

"It's a beautiful night," he sighed, turning his eyes toward the clear starry sky and bright moon.

"Yes." Bel could look only at him, knowing that she had very little time left to do so.

"What did you want to talk about?"

Now that he asked her, she did not really know how to begin. "I . . . well, the other night . . . I wondered whether it—*you*—meant anything by it."

"By what exactly?"

She stared at him, marveling that he could be so dense. Did he really not know what she was referring to? He was not that stupid, she remembered. Was it that he wanted to make her say it? Was he enjoying her discomfort? And why had his attitude towards her changed so much from five minutes ago when he had tried to avoid speaking to her, to now, when he had taken her hand so easily and seemed once again to be declaring his affection for her?

"You kissed me," she reminded him, blushing scarlet.

He looked downcast. "I'm sorry. I shouldn't have done it. It was wrong. You're married. I've seen what infidelity and divorce did to my parents. I shouldn't have let myself get carried away by . . . never mind. Please, could you just forget it?"

She wanted to shout, "No!" The last thing she wanted to do was to forget the warmth and wonder she had felt at receiving genuine tenderness from a man she cared about. It was a memory she would always treasure, one which would sustain her through difficult times ahead, and sometimes remind her that she might still find love and security.

But she nodded, not knowing what else to say, and he seemed satisfied. Now it seemed that, having made his intentions clear, he was in no hurry to return to Haven. Seeing a large rock nearby, he sat and invited her to join him. She did so, delighted to have a little more time alone with him, to enjoy his nearness and his conversation.

"Have you heard from your husband?" he asked.

She grimaced, wishing he had spoken of anything else but that. "No, and I hope not to. I expect he'll be looking for me, and eventually he'll find me, but I hope by then I'll be strong enough to cope with that."

"Why would he come looking for you if he doesn't love you?"

"Anger," she replied simply. "I'm sure he can't bear the thought that I would desert him and take Jake. He'll want to teach me a lesson. He liked to control me. He'll try to drag me home and make my life hell as a penance for thinking about myself instead of his comfort. I know him so well by now I can almost see it happening. Marty will turn up one day out of the blue in his horrible dirty white van, probably with that fat, bald brother of his, both of them baying for blood. But I'll be ready."

Danny seemed disturbed at the thought. "How?"

"I hope to have the divorce underway by then and have someplace decent to live, have some friends nearby perhaps. I'll notify Social Services, find a job, and get my self-confidence back." She thought of Lucy the Labrador and laughed. "Perhaps I'll even get a big dog! Now would you mind if we talked about something else?"

He took a scrap of paper and a pen from his shirt pocket and scribbled down an address and telephone number. "This is the hotel where Steve and I work. They're always looking for staff, and you could live in. The invitation still stands if you want to come to Ireland."

There was nothing she wanted more. It would be far away from Marty and close to Danny, and there would be a home and a job combined. But she noticed that Danny had stopped short of giving her his own address or telephone number, and that his enthusiasm of the other night had waned somewhat. She wondered whether it was right to take Jake overseas. She felt as though she would be abducting her own son, and she feared the repercussions. But she knew she had other options. Wrexham had seemed promising, and there was still Brian's invitation to Scotland, which included a job.

"Thanks," she said noncommittally and accepted the paper without looking at it. "I haven't really decided where to go yet."

He seemed to understand that, wherever she might be this time tomorrow, it would not be with him. He smiled his lazy, enchanting smile and studied her delicate face for a few moments as her eyes lingered longingly over each of his features, then he pulled her to him in a warm hug as though they had been friends for years. She allowed only one tear to fall from beneath her eyelashes onto his strong shoulder, and when they parted she was again confident and composed. They did not speak as they walked back to Haven, knowing that there was only one word left to be said between them, and wanting to save that for tomorrow.

❧

The Hole in the Wall Inn was aptly named on two counts. It nestled obscurely down an alleyway beneath Caernarfon's ancient town walls, its liquor license its sole inducement. It was, as Paul observed, "a hole." The unpolished wooden floor was liberally scattered with sawdust to soak up beer spillages and the occasional less pleasant liquid mess. Its old wobbly wooden tables were sticky and well marked with stained rings and graffiti, and its seats were torn and dirty. But, as Marty responded to his brother, it sold beer, and that was enough to recommend it.

"*Iechyd da,*" Paul said, raising his glass, when they were settled into a dingy corner below a smoke-blackened window. "So, how do we find this guest house?"

Marty stared sullenly at the map and took a long steadying draw on his cigarette. "It's along this road somewhere. I don't know. Ask a policeman?"

Paul wrinkled his nose in disdain. "I'd rather not."

"Yellow Pages?"

That was more like it. Miraculously one was found for them behind the bar, but it gave no further information, just the name and telephone number. "We can't risk phoning them again," Marty said. The barman had no idea where it might be either, so they ordered another round of drinks and then two more, as they sat thoughtfully in the dim bar, trying to work out what to do next.

"You know," Paul said after two hours of fruitless and frustrating contemplation, "if you'd taken better care of that woman, we wouldn't be having to do this."

"What's that supposed to mean?" Marty said, roused from his stupor.

Paul shrugged. "What it sounded like."

"You think I don't know how to look after my wife?"

"You had no control over her, mate. I mean, you let her walk all over you. If you'd let her know her place, she'd never have left."

Marty was angry now. "Like you taught Jan her place? So she left you?"

Paul slammed his pint glass down so hard that his beer slopped out across the table. "I threw that old cow out and don't you forget it!" He wagged a grimy finger close to Marty's scowling face.

Marty indicated his unbelief in this version of events with a single word, at which Paul's finger contracted into a fist and connected heavily with Marty's jaw. The younger man, shocked for only a second, decided that such unbrotherly behavior could not go unpunished and responded with his best right hook.

The police seemed to arrive within only a few minutes, and the fight ended as abruptly as it had begun. The feuding brothers were only too familiar with what might result were they to be charged, and digging into his pocket with his bruised and painful right hand, Marty whisked out his keys.

"It's okay. We're leaving," he barked at the constable as he swept through the door, closely followed by his bleeding brother.

"Not on wheels you're not," the man replied swiftly. "You're in no fit state to drive. Hand over the keys."

"I'm fine!" Marty shrieked.

"Care to prove that?" The constable proffered a Breathalyzer, which Marty regarded with distaste.

"Look, I'm sorry about all this," Paul said in a voice approaching meekness. "We've got somewhere we've got to be rather urgently. We'll be on our way now."

"Hand over the keys. You can have them back at such a time as you can provide a negative breath test at the station. Which, judging by the smell of both of you, will be in about eight hours." Before Marty could say anything more, the constable snatched the keys from his hand, pocketed them, and whipped out a notebook. "Now, I need names and addresses so that I know who to give these back to in the morning."

"Just one thing first," Paul said, pulling himself up to his full height and trying to turn his usual grimace into a smile. "I wonder if you could give us some directions?"

The constable sighed heavily but listened as Paul told him everything they knew about the guest house they sought. "Not that you'll be arriving there tonight," the constable said firmly, "but I think I know the place."

CHAPTER 30

Saturday morning was never easy. It always saddened Gwen to see the suitcases of her guests, who had by now become her friends, pile up in the lounge. She had plenty of work to do, clearing the dining room and readying the guest house for an entirely new set of visitors, but she liked to linger over the good-byes, commit to memory each face, and assure each guest that they would always be welcome at Haven.

As always, Edward busied himself helping to carry the bags to the cars, although there was little assistance needed on this occasion. Bel Hunt had very little luggage, Danny O'Hanlon and Steve Collins were more than capable of carrying their own, and Angela and Stuart were now staying a few more days. As he bent to pick up a large package wrapped in brown paper that was leaning against Brian McNaught's suitcase, however, he was stopped by the quiet and apologetic voice of the Scotsman. "I don't think I'll take those with me," he said.

Edward straightened in surprise. "Aren't these your paintings?"

Brian nodded and picked them up carefully, laying the parcel on the coffee table in the center of the room where he proceeded to remove the paper covering the pictures. Gently he lifted the wood-mounted canvasses out of their wrappings and laid them face-up for all to see. Gwen hurried over, fascinated. She had not seen the completed painting of Haven.

As she looked at it, she was amazed that Brian had managed in just a small space to convey the timelessness and endless expanse of the landscape, with sweeping brush strokes drawing the eye across the wild mountains and down to the focal point of the still lake, its depth and tranquility perfectly captured. In the foreground every tiny detail of the stone farmhouse was lovingly picked out. Although Gwen had not hitherto appreciated this view of the plainer back of her home as it nestled into the mountainside, she saw a new beauty in it through this representation. It was a stunning picture, perfectly capturing all that she most loved about this place.

Brian blushed at her ready compliments and simply said, "I'd like you to have it."

Gwen dragged her eyes from the picture to Brian's face and saw that he was in earnest. Nevertheless, she had to ask, "Are you quite sure?"

Brian simply nodded; apparently no other explanation was required. Gwen was sorry that he had already paid his bill; she would have liked to repay his kindness with a considerable discount.

"It will look wonderful above our fireplace," Edward said. "Thank you so much, Mr. McNaught. It is a very generous gift. We are extremely grateful."

Brian seemed rather embarrassed and quickly turned to Bel, who was also admiring the painting from the far side of the room. "Belinda, would you like to take the other one?"

Bel looked at him in astonishment. "The Criccieth Castle painting? Oh, no, I really couldn't—it's so beautiful. It wouldn't be right—"

"I'd like you to have it," Brian insisted. "Your son is in it, after all, and you did see it being created."

"But Steve and Danny are in it too. It wouldn't be fair to them . . ."

"Take it," Steve said. "It's nice, but we're not much into these things. Besides, we haven't got our own homes to hang it in. You have it."

Bel nodded finally, smiling at Brian. "You are such a kind and generous man, and a talented one. I will treasure it always because it will remind me of this week and of you. Thank you."

Brian was smiling with genuine happiness, and Gwen was pleased to see it. He really seemed to have gained pleasure from creating and giving these exquisite gifts, and he seemed so much more at ease and content than when he had first arrived at Haven. At the beginning, she had not been certain whether she even liked him, but now that she understood him better, she sincerely hoped he would continue to recover his emotional health and soon be restored as the loyal and thoughtful man that she now knew him to be. Perhaps she and Edward had been able to help a little in that process, and she knew that Belinda Hunt somehow had. But the week was at an end, and it was time for all her dear guests to go back to their homes and their everyday lives.

⚜

Danny and Steve were the first to leave. Flinging their bags into the car and blowing wild kisses at all those who watched from the doorway, they sped away, the air full of noise from the powerful engine, loud music, and barking dog.

As the car flew down the drive at speeds others might have called dangerous, Danny felt a lump in his throat at what he was leaving behind. When Steve and he had first arrived, they hadn't a thought in the world except to enjoy themselves, and yet now everything seemed so much more complex and disturbing. He had seen Bel's pain and it had shaken his youthful, carefree spirit, reminding him that the world was not always fair. It had also awakened in him a desire to protect and care for those who did not have his self-confidence and good fortune. He was traveling in a reliable car to a ferry that would return him to his comfortable home, but Bel had only a battered old car that might only last a few more miles, a case of clothes, and her son. She had no guarantees, no certainty in her future. His concern for her and his admiration of her courage had matured him, he realized, but at the same time he almost wished that he had never met her. He might now spend the rest of his life wondering what had become of her and never have any hope of knowing.

At the bottom of the drive, Steve drove more carefully, edging the car out so that he could see a little further round the corners. Just as he had concluded it was safe to pull out and stepped on the gas, however, a battered white van suddenly flew around the bend and blocked his path. It screeched to a halt, indicator light suddenly blinking wildly.

The two cars were close enough that the driver of the van was clearly visible to the occupants of the car. He was a burly man in his early forties perhaps, stern-faced and with little hair remaining, his face newly cut and bruised. His eyes were fixed on the sign beside the driveway, which read "Haven—Bed and Breakfast." The passenger looked similar enough to be his brother but was perhaps ten years younger. He had a little more hair, at any rate, and his face might be quite handsome but for the same scowling expression. His feet rested on the dashboard, revealing muddy boots, the soles of which were pressed against the windscreen.

Steve maneuvered awkwardly out into the roadway, allowing just enough space for the van to crawl past and wincing when it seemed that it might scrape his precious paintwork. When the van began laboring up the drive, Steve muttered something derogatory under his breath, straightened the car out and sped away again.

Something bothered Danny about that van, as though it should mean something to him, and yet he just couldn't place it… Trying to force the nagging feeling that the van and its occupants were important in some way, he turned his mind back to their little wager and turned to Steve.

"Time for you to pay up, mate."

Steve feigned ignorance. "Pay up? For what?"

"We had a bet, remember? First one to discover Bel Hunt's big secret?"

"And you did?"

Danny shrugged. "She's running away from her husband."

Steve snorted. "Even I figured out that much."

"His name is Marty. They'd been married for five years, and he lives in Sussex. Now stop trying to weasel out of it and pay up."

Steve sighed heavily and craned his neck round to look at the dog in the back seat, not the safest maneuver while driving, but it was sometimes the only way to let her know he was talking to her. "Lucy, you're Danny's dog again, okay? You go home with Danny today." Focusing back on the road, he swerved back to the left hand side just in time to avoid a Fiat driven by an irate-looking elderly man. "I'll win her back again, just you wait," he muttered. "And then we'll have to start betting money. I'm fed up with having to part with my dog."

Unable to shake a strange feeling of unease, Danny searched his consciousness. Something was wrong, he knew, and his brain suddenly connected two images: the first of a pale and fearful Bel telling him about Marty's brother and an old white van, predicting that the men would come looking for her; the second of the two surly-looking men in a white van, which Steve's car had passed at the bottom of Haven's driveway.

The more he thought about it, the more certain he became that the two men in the van had come to drag Bel back to the terrifying world she had escaped. He tried to push that thought out of his mind, convince himself that they were innocent tourists, or perhaps workmen come to fix Haven's drains. After all, lots of people drove white vans.

Back home, back to normality, Danny thought, back to his life. He shouldn't worry about Bel, he should forget her now that she was in his past. But it wasn't quite that simple; he wasn't the same carefree person he had been last week. The thought of those two angry men in the van and the fear that had found Bel dug at his conscience. He fought it for a whole minute, then finally shouted, "Steve, stop the car!"

CHAPTER 31

The knock on the door came so soon after the lively young men had left that Gwen's initial thought was that they had forgotten something and returned. She was a little alarmed then, on opening the door, to see not Steve and Danny's grinning faces, but those of two older men, both twisted into expressions of bitter rage, the kind of which Gwen had rarely encountered. Edward was immediately at her side.

"I'm looking," said the younger of the two, speaking slowly as though she were stupid, "for my wife."

Before Gwen could even think of a response, there was a sharp gasp from Bel and Jake's pitiful voice cried, "It's Dad!" as the child dived behind his mother and clung to her legs as if trying to hide. Both men peered past Gwen and Edward, then, seeing Bel, roughly pushed them aside and strode into the room. They stopped just short of Bel, who seemed even thinner and more vulnerable against their bulk, but whose expression was one of resoluteness, despite her pale complexion. Gwen felt suddenly cold and closed the door.

"Good morning, Lindy," the man said, speaking with an exaggerated evenness that did not hide the acidity behind the words. "I thought I might find you here."

"Marty," she acknowledged coldly but said nothing more. It was Bel's husband, Gwen realized, and shuddered as she began to understand what the young woman had suffered and why she had been forced to leave.

"I hope you've enjoyed your little break, but it's time for you to come home now." He put a firm and heavy hand on her shoulder, and she flinched, disgust evident in her face. "Look, stop this nonsense. I'm sorry if I did something to upset you, but whatever this silly business is all about, we can forget about it. I'm prepared to forgive you for what you've done."

"What I've done?" Her voice was weak and high-pitched.

"In running away and taking my boy." He had barely acknowledged the presence of his son until that moment, Gwen noted. "I might not have been a perfect husband, but I can change. Let's forget this ever happened and get back to normal." Gwen had seen genuine repentance before. It was always stirring and poignant, and it inspired hope. This wasn't it.

Bel took a step back. "I don't want to get back to *normal*. I don't want to go home." She was close to tears, Gwen thought and wondered how many years of bullying it had taken to reduce an attractive, confident woman to this defeated, fearful creature. Bel had suffered enough not only in her marriage, but just in these last few minutes. Gwen had seen the tears in her eyes as she said good-bye to Danny, had noticed that she clasped her hands firmly behind her back as though to stop herself reaching for him, and her heart had gone out to her once again. Now to be faced so soon with Danny's opposite and the object of her greatest fear and loathing was more than she should be expected to bear.

Edward spoke up. "I think we should all discuss this. Would you gentlemen like to sit down for a moment and have a cup of tea?"

"There's nothing to discuss. It's none of your business," the older one growled, his voice husky from a lifetime of smoking.

"I think you'll find it is our business."

Gwen was amazed to find that it was Brian who had spoken, his voice louder and stronger than she had ever heard it. He had even stepped forward and placed himself between Bel and her odious husband.

"Why? What's it to do with you?" barked Marty.

"I'm her lawyer," Brian replied evenly, meeting the angry man's gaze and proffering his card. "You'll be hearing from me shortly with regard to a restraining order and the divorce."

Marty, confused momentarily, looked at the card but did not take it, and finally said, "Well, until I do hear from you officially, you can keep out of it!"

"Sorry, I'm not prepared to do that," Brian said, his voice as steady as before. "Now why don't you just leave?"

"She's my wife!" Marty shouted. "She belongs with me! You want a bit, old man, you get yourself your own woman." He pushed Brian roughly out of the way, only to find him replaced by Stuart Kirby, equally as fearless in his defense of the young woman they had all come to admire and care for. Angela, Gwen noticed, was hurrying her children into the kitchen, away from the confrontation, and that gave her an idea. She cut into the noisy argument with all the boldness she could muster and prayed as she did so that the other guests might understand her plan and not protest at her words.

"Well, Belinda has to pay before she goes home anyway. We need to settle that in the *office*. Will you come with me, my dear?" She didn't have an office, as her guests would know perfectly well. Perhaps that might indicate to them that she was plotting something.

Bel turned to look at her, wide-eyed, her brow furrowed in a combination of surprise and puzzlement. Gwen nodded desperately, earnestly, at her, and Bel picked up her handbag and looked toward her husband.

"Go and pay your bill," he grunted. For a moment Gwen feared that he might suggest his brother accompany her, or that Jake stay in the lounge with them, but Brian, Stuart, and Edward had engaged the bigger man in a heated argument, and Marty didn't seem bright enough to have guessed at Gwen's plan. They were able to leave the room without being challenged, Bel clutching her frightened son's hand as they almost ran into the kitchen. Angela was there, somehow managing to protectively clasp two children and a baby on her lap, her look both worried and sympathetic.

"Now go!" Gwen whispered urgently to Bel, indicating the back door. "The men may be able to distract them for a few more minutes. Have you got your car keys? Good. Your luggage is in the car—just drive off as quickly as you can. With luck you'll be long gone before they realize what's happened."

Bel stared in wonder at Gwen. "But . . . my bill. I have to pay—like you said . . ."

"No time for that! Don't worry about it. Just go! And when you arrive at wherever you're going, write to me and I'll send your painting on to you."

Bel wasted precious seconds looking in overwhelmed gratitude and love at Gwen, and then hugging her tightly. Then without another word, and holding her finger to her lips to indicate to Jake that he should be as quiet as possible, Belinda Hunt left through the back door and did not stop to look back.

Angela and Gwen watched her go, and without a word passing between them, they both strained to hear the sound of the car over the raised voices in the lounge. When, five minutes later, they had still heard nothing, they tentatively walked through the back door and around the side path. Bel's rusty old car was gone. She must have let it coast down the drive, Gwen surmised, rather than risk drawing attention to her escape by starting the engine. She admired Bel's bravery and cleverness and said a quiet prayer to speed her safely on her way.

A moment later the front door burst open and the two men flew out, words Gwen would have preferred not to hear issuing from their mouths as they saw what had happened. She herself was the object of some of those curses, but she resolutely held the gaze of the angry men, knowing that Bel was safe, free again, and that Edward, Stuart, and Brian would not let any harm come to Gwen.

"Where is she going?" the bigger man asked menacingly.

Gwen was able to reply with complete and transparent honesty, "I don't know."

"We can still catch her," Marty said, wrenching open the door of the van. His brother seemed to agree, and within seconds they had both gone, the wheels of the van spinning and throwing up stones as it pulled away. The oppressive atmosphere lifted and there was a collective sigh of relief. Edward kissed Gwen as he congratulated her on her quick action for Bel.

"Could they really catch her up?" Angela said, worried.

Gwen sighed. "She's got a few minutes' head start, but I really don't know. Let's pray that they don't."

CHAPTER 32

S teve was becoming increasingly impatient as he sat in the powerful car parked at the side of the road, waiting for his friend to wrestle with his conscience and decide whether or not to turn back and help Bel. They had a boat to catch and time was short, and what did Danny imagine he could possibly do to help anyway? Steve turned up the volume on the stereo and drummed his fingers on the steering wheel in time with the music. He had some sympathy with his friend's dilemma. He had quite liked the girl, too, although evidently not as much as Danny did. It couldn't be easy for him, wondering what she was going through.

In a second their situation changed. As Steve stared wistfully at the road ahead, a battered and rusty old car drove past them, its blonde occupant wearing a cautious smile, and then disappeared round the next bend. "That was her!" Steve cried.

"Bel?" Danny asked tentatively, as though not daring hope for as much.

"Yes, and the little lad, and she was smiling."

Danny's jaunty grin returned, even wider than usual, and he patted his friend on the back. "Great, well, let's get on our way then."

With relief Steve slammed the gear lever into place and downed the gas pedal, and the black car sped away. The road was narrow here and twisted and turned as it negotiated rocks and boundaries, and with each bend the young men looked hopefully ahead wondering whether they had caught up with Bel, yet she always seemed to be just out of sight. When Danny heard Steve gasp, he searched the road before them, thinking he must have spotted Bel's car, but Steve's face was tense.

At his terse comment, "Behind us," Danny looked over his shoulder and took in a sharp breath. Close behind them, so close that they could clearly see the fury on the faces of the driver and passenger, was the dirty white van they knew Bel to be fleeing from. Even as he watched, it accelerated and pulled yet closer to them, until Danny could not see the front radiator. Obviously they wanted to go faster; they wanted to overtake and catch Bel. He could not let that happen.

"Steve, drive as slowly as you can. Don't let them pass! She hasn't got enough of a lead. We need to buy her some more time!"

Biting his lip in anguish, fully aware of the dangerous proximity of the van behind them, Steve gently tapped the brake, then a little more, each time bracing himself against the crunch he felt sure would come as the front fender of the vehicle behind connected with his precious car. They were furious he could see, the younger one bashing the dashboard with his fist, the driver swerving perilously as he pulled out to try and see past the black sports car, but each time had to pull back as they entered yet another blind bend. After three long agonizing minutes, Steve noticed with alarm that there was a small straight stretch of road ahead and no vehicles in the opposite lane. He heard the van revving in anticipation, and holding his breath in fear, he pulled the wheel round so that they straddled the white line in the middle of the road, closing his ears against the angry hooting of the horn and his mind to the possibility that they might try to squeeze past anyway. His paintwork was perfect, but they had nothing to lose in a little scrape. He was doing barely twenty-five miles per hour on a stretch where sixty would be both easy and legal, and his only comfort was that he still could not see Bel's car ahead.

Mercifully the road soon returned to its narrow bends and tight turns, and Steve began protesting to Danny that his car was unused to driving so slowly, that before long the men in the car behind them would lose patience and push them out of the way. Danny, white and yet determined, merely insisted he keep the speed as low as possible. The junction was five miles ahead, if Bel could reach it well before them, then the men she was fleeing would be unable to see which road she chose, unable to follow her any further. She just needed more space and more time.

But time had run out. The two men in the second car had reached the end of their patience. Before Steve had a chance to respond, the driver had pulled alongside them on a sharp right bend and was attempting to overtake them, despite the absence of a clear view of the road ahead. As the van drew even with the black car, Danny looked at the two men, seeing their rage, and the obscene gestures with which they made it doubly clear.

But Steve saw nothing except the huge red tractor chugging peacefully towards them in the opposite lane. He cried out as he slammed his right foot to the floor, hoping desperately to speed them to safety. The car, powerful and obedient, especially in such low gear, leapt ahead as though stung and flew past the tractor at precisely the same moment that the van swerved to avoid it. In terror at knowing what the next few seconds would certainly bring, Steve and Danny braced themselves for the expected sound of impact from behind them. Even so, they were unprepared for the shattering sound of the van colliding with the stone wall alongside the road, spinning round and presenting its high sides to the unrelenting strength of the tractor.

⚜

Two miles ahead of them, Bel happily sang nursery rhymes to her contented child as the rusty old car paced out the miles to her new life. She was triumphant, free! She caught sight of herself in the wing mirror and smiled. Her hair was glossy and attractively tossed by the wind blowing through the open window, her eyes sparkled, and her skin had lost its sallowness and now shone with health and sported a light, glowing tan. Had she gained a little weight, too? Gwen Anderton's cooking was superb; she could not remember ever eating so well.

Entirely oblivious of the dramatic events in her wake, she smiled as she considered the three doors that lay ahead of her, which held some promise for a safe and hopeful future. First, there was Wrexham, which offered real independence and opportunity. Although close to the border, it was still in the country she had come to love so much over the last week. And, second, there was Brian's offer to work for him. She thought it would be good to live somewhere where she already had a good friend, and somewhere so very far from her old home. And third, there was Ireland. As Bel reflected on the temptations of Ireland, she thought fondly of Danny and Steve, unaware that in the months and years to come, their thoughts of her would be a combination of admiration tinged with guilt for their role in the accident. They felt fairly safe in assuming that the tractor driver was probably uninjured . . . but were not as sure of the fate of the two brutish men.

She sighed happily, luxuriating in the many possibilities on the horizon before her. There remained a little more time in which to make her decision. The crossroads was still five miles away.

Brian McNaught left soon after Bel, quietly shaking hands with his host and hostess and even smiling when Gwen commented that his wife must have missed him. "I've missed her," he admitted. "But I think she needed the break from me as much as I needed to get away."

"I hope you're feeling better for this week's holiday," Gwen said earnestly.

He thought about that. "A little. Mostly I feel more hopeful, and I can begin to see a time when I might be well again. Thank you so much for giving me the time and space I needed. This is an incredible place."

She could not help but agree. She marveled that he had changed so much and had even managed to speak so freely and easily to her. She waved and waved as the Volvo drew away from the house, and reflected that she had yet another needy soul to pray for daily.

She turned away from the window at last. There was still so much work to do to prepare Haven for the new guests, but it had been a long and stressful morning and it was time for a rest, she decided.

The harsh ring of the telephone broke into her thoughts, and she answered it with her usual greeting, her voice cheerful and light.

"Let me speak to Angela," a curt voice demanded.

Taken aback for a moment, Gwen asked who was calling and was told, as she had suspected, that it was Ian Anderton. She hesitated, trying to decide whether it might be best to speak to him or simply pass the phone to Angela. She eventually decided on the former.

"It's good to hear from you, Ian. How are you? We're sorry you couldn't make it this week."

Ian's cultivated accent betrayed none of its Midlands roots as he replied in a tone of ice, "I don't want to speak to you. I want to speak to Angela. But while I've got you on the line, perhaps you could explain exactly what black magic you worked to make her want to stay there longer than she has to? I had a postcard this morning . . . Am I now the only one in my family who sees you for what you really are?"

Gwen bit her lip, fighting back tears and feeling the color drain from her cheeks, and wordlessly handed the phone to Angela. Edward saw her distress and was at her side immediately, putting a comforting arm around her shoulder.

"Just as I thought everything was perfect," Gwen sighed as they listened to Angela's efforts to persuade her brother that she was not the evil temptress he imagined. So recently converted from the same opinion herself, Angela's arguments were not as fervent as they might be, but Gwen had heard the bitterness in Ian's voice and knew that it would take far more than his sister's assurances, however enthusiastically they might be offered, to change Ian's opinion of her character. Having been faced with two different types of anger today, she imagined she preferred brutish rage to refined cruelty, but she knew that Ian's words had been the more hurtful because she so badly wanted him to accept her.

"He'll come round in the end," Edward assured her, clearly unhappy with his son for upsetting Gwen on what had already been a stressful day at the end of a difficult week. Gwen managed a smile, which brightened when Angela gave up trying to argue with her brother, replaced the phone, and told Gwen to ignore him as he had always been the stubborn one.

Gwen settled down beside Edward on the sofa and tried to put Ian out of her mind by feasting her eyes with considerable satisfaction on the beautiful painting which still lay on the coffee table. There was so much to enjoy and look forward to. She and her husband had to finish planning their visit to Salt Lake; there was a great deal they wanted to do during their time there, and so many old friends and returned missionaries to visit. Stuart played with young Adam on the floor, and Angela smiled as she listened to her child's happy laughter and the excitement of her father and his new wife as they talked together about the trip.

Gwen seemed to be looking forward to seeing all the shops. Angela had not imagined that Gwen might enjoy window shopping as she did, but there was much she had to learn about this kind-hearted and honest woman. There were so few shops in this rural area that perhaps Gwen didn't often get the chance to enjoy browsing the sales. Angela wondered whether she and Gwen might go shopping together one day in Birmingham, and wished briefly that she could be there to help her choose her wedding dress.

Edward was looking forward to experiencing a different culture, and Gwen laughed when he said how much he wanted to try traditional American food and Angela said she would take him to the new McDonald's restaurant in Caernarfon. Most of all, though, they were looking forward to attending the temple together, the wonder clear in their expressions as they spoke of what it would mean to them to know that they were sealed together forever. As Angela watched them and saw the love plain in their faces, she knew at last how happy her father was to be living with Gwen in the peace and sanctity of Haven.

EPILOGUE

My dear Bel,

I can't tell you how happy Edward and I were on returning from our visit to the USA to find your letter waiting for us and to know that our prayers for you have been answered. I am enclosing this letter with your beautiful painting which I hope will remind you of your stay here every time you look at it.

It is good to hear that you are settled in Scotland and that Jake is enjoying school and Brian will soon be ready to start work again—and with you as his secretary! I am sure you will prove a great help and support to him just as he has been to you these last few weeks. Will you be taking up his wife's offer to collect Jake from school and look after him until you get back from work? It seems easier than doing part-time hours, and don't forget there are the school holidays to consider, too. She sounds a very kind person, and I am sure she will love having a young child about the house again. How fortunate that they have a guest room in their home, which will save you having to find somewhere of your own, at least for a while.

It is kind of Brian to agree to handle your divorce. I know it cannot have been an easy decision, but in this case I do feel you are justified in taking it. I wonder why your husband is taking so long to reply? We had a postcard today from some shared friends—Danny and Steve wrote to thank me for an enjoyable week and asked me to write to them immediately if there was anything they should know about. They seemed particularly anxious. I think they did a great deal of growing up while they were here, and perhaps the process has continued since. It seems odd, too, that they should wait over a month before writing to me, but perhaps they remembered that we would be away.

Edward and I had the most wonderful three weeks in America we could have imagined. Our sealing was the high point, of course. A few days beforehand, my old friend Megan, with whom we were staying, took me shopping for a really special dress. Since I was a young girl I have dreamed of marrying in a beautiful white dress in the temple. Even so, seeing Edward smiling at me, I forgot all about the white silk and lace dress and the incredible beauty of the sealing room in the Salt Lake Temple, even the amazing spirit surrounding us. I could only think how wonderful it was that I was going to be with Edward for eternity. It is hard to find words to describe it all, but it has changed us both for the better.

We were also able to attend general conference, which was another wonderful spiritual experience, and still found plenty of time to see all the tourist sites. Utah is very beautiful, but I was homesick for my green hills and rain!

I am still laughing at the image of you, when the missionaries tracted your street, reciting the Book of Mormon to them! They must have been so astonished! But it is wonderful that you, as well as Brian and Fiona, are having the discussions. Do think and pray carefully about everything the missionaries tell you.

Please pass our good wishes on to Brian and Fiona. I am so ashamed that I mistook Brian's shyness for rudeness when he first arrived at Haven, but now I have to admire his bravery and kindness. Edward joins me in wishing you and Jake all the very best for the future and we will continue to remember you in our prayers.

> *Pob bendith,*
> *Gwen Anderton*

ABOUT THE AUTHOR

Anna Jones was born and brought up in the south of England but went to Wales to study English at the University of Wales and never quite got around to going home again. It was there that she met her husband, Ioan, and also came into contact with The Church of Jesus Christ of Latter-day Saints. She now lives in the seaside town of Criccieth, with her husband and two daughters, Gwenllian and Angharad.

Anna enjoys rock music, science fiction, and her computer. She works part-time for a lawyer assistance program that helps the Brian McNaughts of this world. Her first novel, *Haven,* was also published by Covenant Communications, Inc.

She would love to hear from her readers, who can email her at **anna@annajones.org.uk.** She also has a website at **www.annajones.org.uk.**

Love Lights the Way

Prologue

It was the most important day of her life and Ashlyn felt like throwing up.

A formation of butterflies swooped and swirled inside her stomach. She glanced at the clock again. Someone should have come and taken her to the sealing room by now. She and Jake were already fifteen minutes late for their scheduled sealing time. The temple was booked solid in June and the temple workers kept a tight schedule.

Something was wrong.

Heavenly Father, please bless us so that everything will be okay. I'm so nervous. Please help me calm down. Bless me with Thy spirit so I can enjoy this wonderful experience. And thank you for Jake. He's the most wonderful man in the world.

The prayer helped a little, but she couldn't calm the queasiness in her middle.

She didn't dare sit for fear of crushing the satiny smooth fabric of her wedding dress, so instead, she paced the floor. Running her fingers across the dozens of pearls handsewn to the lacy bodice of the dress, Ashlyn tried to steady her breathing and relax, and force the awful thoughts away that kept clouding her mind.

She glanced in one of the dozens of mirrors in the bride's room of the Salt Lake Temple and checked her reflection for the hundredth time. Adjusting the neckline of her wedding gown, she turned sideways, pulled in her stomach, and straightened her shoulders. Then, with a sigh, she exhaled and began pacing again.

Everything's going to be okay, she told herself.

Soon, she would kneel at the altar, across from her fiancé, Jake Gerrard, and seal their love for time and all eternity. The thought sent her heart aflutter. No one had ever made her feel the way he made her feel, and she looked forward to spending forever with him. With Jake life was exciting and full of surprises, and she knew that life with him could never be boring. He was spontaneous, wild and crazy, and passionate about life. He wanted to live every day to its fullest and enjoy every minute. He was her handsome knight in shining armor.

But aside from his good looks and witty sense of humor, he had a deep, thoughtful side of him that Ashlyn found mysterious and intriguing, which explained how—only three short, romantic, and magical months after meeting him—they were now getting married. Jake said he loved her and couldn't live without her. She had never felt this way about anyone.

Her mother and stepfather had expressed their concern about her marrying Jake, but Ashlyn felt their concerns were unwarranted. They worried about her marrying someone who had dropped out of college and who didn't yet have a steady job. Even more, they were concerned that Jake didn't have any income or savings to provide for his wife after they were married. But Ashlyn had put some money away, and with her degree in journalism and a teaching certificate, she could help support them until Jake decided what he wanted to do.

Ashlyn knew it would be difficult, but she and Jake would make things work. That's what marriage was all about. There were many challenges ahead for them, but with Jake by her side, Ashlyn wasn't afraid.

They planned to honeymoon in Cozumel. Ashlyn had wanted to go to Hawaii, but Jake had assured her that Cozumel was even better. When they returned, they would move to Arizona since Jake liked the warmer climate and thought he might attend ASU. Ashlyn had just secured a job for the fall teaching English at a Salt Lake junior high school, but she knew she could find work in Arizona. Jake had already gone to Arizona to find them an apartment, and their belongings were packed in their new Land Cruiser. Since Jake had thought the larger vehicle would be more practical for them, Ashlyn had sold her Honda Accord. Besides, a Land Cruiser was a real "man's" car,

Jake insisted. With their plans made, they were all set for their new life together.

As she paced, Ashlyn thought about their first meeting. It had been at a Young Adult fireside. He'd caught her eye the minute he walked through the door into the chapel. It was a multi-stake fireside and she'd never seen him before. After the fireside, with a little effort and some finagling, she'd managed to line up behind him in the refreshment line. It was love at first sight for both of them.

They had struck up a casual conversation, which had led to a lunch date the next day. After that they saw each other every day. Within several weeks they'd confessed their love for each other and Jake had proposed.

Now they were getting married.

At least, they were supposed to be getting married. Ashlyn checked the clock again.

What in the world was going on?

She wondered if something had happened to Jake. She knew he was at the temple because they'd arrived at the same time. They'd spoken briefly. He seemed nervous and quiet, but then she was nervous, too. After all, this was their big day.

Maybe he was sick. But if he were, surely someone would have told her by now.

Finally, she couldn't stand it any longer. She had to know what was going on.

Opening the door a crack, she heard several people talking down the hall. Recognizing her mother's and stepfather's voices, she left the room to join them and find out what was causing the delay. Just when she was about to turn the corner, the mention of Jake's name caught her attention, and she stopped cold.

"I just don't know how to tell her." It was her mother's voice. "This is going to break her heart."

Ashlyn's breath caught in her chest, and a sick feeling washed over her. What was going to break her heart? What was her mother talking about?

"I'll tell her, if you want me to," her stepfather offered.

"No," her mother said softly. "I think it would be best coming from me."

"We're so sorry." The elderly voice was unfamiliar, no doubt one of the male workers at the temple. "We don't see this happen too often."

"I think I should go with you, Miranda." Ashlyn recognized the voice of Jake's mother, Barbara.

"No!" Miranda's voice came sharply. "That will just make it more painful."

Ashlyn felt tears sting her eyes. A knot formed in her throat. Backing up to the wall, she leaned against it for support. She felt faint. Something had happened to Jake.

"What are you going to say?" Garrett, her stepfather, asked.

"I don't know," Miranda cried. "How do I tell my daughter her fiancé has changed his mind and doesn't want to marry her?"

For a moment Ashlyn was stunned, not sure that she heard her mother right. Her face and hands tingled, then went numb. Then the words slowly seeped in until they speared her consciousness with a white heat. Jake had changed his mind?

He didn't want to marry her?

Suddenly the walls started melting, and the floor began to spin. Ashlyn felt her knees go weak, then everything went black.

CHAPTER 1

Ten months later

"You didn't get the job," the woman on the phone told Ashlyn. "We hired another teacher who had more experience. I'm sorry."

Ashlyn hung up the phone with a frustrated sigh. She was tired of going to interviews and not getting hired. What was she doing wrong? She'd been offered a job once; the principal had believed her capable despite her lack of experience. But now it seemed that no one would even give her chance.

Her mother, Miranda Erickson, burst through the garage door with both hands full of grocery bags, which she deposited on the counter. Seeing the look on her daughter's face, Miranda knew instinctively that something was the matter. "What's wrong, honey?"

"I just got a call from Oakdale Elementary. They hired someone else." Ashlyn tried to speak casually, but she couldn't stop the tears that stung her eyes.

"I'm sorry, sweetie." Miranda walked over to her daughter and gave her a hug. "You'll get a job," she assured her. "You can't give up."

"Mom," Ashlyn said sharply, "that was the last opening. There are no other teaching positions available."

Miranda winced at her daughter's tone but kept her voice calm and patient. "Something will work out," she said, trying to sound positive. "You'll see."

But Ashlyn didn't believe her. Nothing had worked out for the last ten months. It was as if Jake deserting her at the temple had somehow jinxed the rest of her life.

Hoping to brighten the mood, Miranda said, "We got a letter today from Adam." Adam was Ashlyn's younger brother, who was on a mission in Portugal. He was loving every minute of it and would be home in only five more months. He and his companion had just baptized a father and mother and their two daughters.

Ashlyn listened as her mother described Adam's letter. "That's great," she said, trying to be excited for him. But she was too miserable to feel anything but sorry for herself.

Miranda made a last attempt to brighten her daughter's mood. "Hey, you didn't tell me what Camryn had to say when she called the other day. How's she doing?"

Camryn Davenport was Ashlyn's roommate from college at Southern Utah University. After a year at the University of Utah, Ashlyn had moved with friends to Cedar City in southern Utah to go to SUU, wanting the chance to live away from home and be on her own for a while. Camryn was there on scholarship and had been assigned to their dorm. She and Ashlyn had quickly become friends, and they'd grown very close. So close that Camryn would also have been Ashlyn's maid of honor, had her wedding actually taken place. Now Cami only had one more month of school before she graduated in interior design. Ashlyn didn't know how she would've made it through the last ten months without her friend.

"She's coming up to spend Easter vacation with us," Ashlyn said. "She said something about checking out the job market while she's here. I would love it if she moved to Salt Lake. Hopefully she'll have better luck finding a job than I have."

That night as Ashlyn pulled on her pajamas, she thought about her friend. She'd missed Cami and all the fun they'd had as roommates. There was nothing like a midnight run to Albertson's for Twinkies and red licorice, or Cami's interior design projects, one which had cost the girls their cleaning deposit on the apartment. They never did find out how that fire had started.

Ashlyn's gaze traveled to the corner of her room where her wedding bouquet of baby pink and powder blue roses, now shriveled and dried, hung on her wall, above a stack of boxes containing china, towels, and other trousseau items she'd collected in anticipation of her marriage to Jake Gerrard. Her mother had tried many times to get Ashlyn to put everything away and to move on with her life, but Ashlyn felt her mother just didn't understand. Just because Jake had stopped loving her didn't mean she had stopped loving him. Ashlyn wasn't sure why, but for some reason she needed to have those things close to her. She often stayed up late at night, looking through her scrapbooks and the proofs of her engagement pictures.

Picking up one of her wedding announcements, she read for at least the hundredth time the announcement that had never come to pass.

Dr. and Mrs. David L. Gerrard
are pleased to announce the marriage of their son
Jacob Ryan Gerrard
to
Ashlyn Kensington
daughter of the late Thomas Kensington
and Garrett and Miranda Erickson.

Ashlyn wondered where Jake was, what he was doing. She'd only seen him twice in the last ten months. The first time had been on that same day he stood her up at the temple. He'd come to her house to tell her why he'd changed his mind.

"I just couldn't do it," he said, his voice a dull monotone. "I thought I loved you, but when it came down to being married for eternity, I realized I wasn't ready. It wouldn't be fair to you and it wouldn't be fair to me."

Ashlyn couldn't even respond. She'd cried the entire time he was there and for the entire week afterward. She never wanted to show her face in public again. Her heart and spirit were shattered and her pride obliterated. She felt hollow and empty inside. Many times she wondered if she would ever recover; most days she doubted it.

The one other time she'd seen him was at a University of Utah football game. Jake hadn't seen her, but she'd watched him through her stepdad's binoculars. He sat with a bunch of friends, some guys, some girls. The group appeared to be having a great time, and seeing him so happy, so obviously "over" her, seemed to reopen her wounds and rub salt into them. Which was probably the reason she didn't like to go out anymore; she didn't want to run into him again. She knew she couldn't handle it—especially if he was with another girl.

She put the wedding announcement down, then touched the feathery softness of the quill pen that guests would have used to sign their names in the wedding registry. Shutting her eyes, she remembered how hard it had been to return all the gifts that had arrived prior to the wedding day. The look of pity on people's faces when they saw her in church or ran into her at the grocery store nearly killed her. It was easier to avoid people than endure those "looks" or their questions.

She couldn't imagine going on with the rest of her life like this. At the same time she didn't know how to get over Jake. He'd left an enormous hole in her heart when he walked out on her. How would she ever repair it and go on with her life?